Angus MacDonald has lived all his life in the Highlands and is steeped in its history. He built up several successful businesses before changing his career to write the Ardnish trilogy, open a large bookshop and build the Highland Cinema in Fort William.

D1343040

Praise for *We Fought for Ardnish*, Part 3 of the Ardnish series

'An intense and bittersweet love story ... the descriptions of travel from Italy to Canada and the Italian front combine to make this a compelling and engaging story'
Scottish Field

'A captivating novel ... which incorporates so much of the beautiful Highland scene and its people alongside the horrors and destruction of a war-torn world. An inspiring read'
The Braes

'Not only a gripping and at times horrifying adventure ... it is also an important piece of social history. But perhaps above all, it is a tale of the importance of true love and determination'
Scots Magazine

'An excellent reflection of love of one's home and heritage. A page turner'
Oban Times

'A haunting salute to a past way of life and a testament to the timeless values of loyalty, faith and family'
National Post

Ardnish

ANGUS MACDONALD

BIRLINN

First published in 2020 by
Birlinn Limited
West Newington House
10 Newington Road
Edinburgh
EH9 1QS

www.birlinn.co.uk

ISBN: 978 1 78027 651 9

British Library Cataloguing-in-Publication Data
A catalogue record for this book is
available from the British Library

Typeset by Hewer Text UK Ltd, Edinburgh
Printed and bound by Clays Ltd, Elcograf S.p.A.

To my wonderful cousins, the Miramichi MacDonalds, whose forebears emigrated to Cape Breton in 1824 from the West Highlands of Scotland. They have introduced me to New Scotland and shown me that the ties that bind families to their homeland, and to each other, are strong.

Acknowledgements

My father, Rory MacDonald, has been the inspiration for the Ardnish trilogy, but I also owe thanks to my ancestors, Col. Willie MacDonald and his son Andrew, who fought in the Boer War, and in the First and Second World Wars, and sent a treasure trove of letters home. Their regiment, the Lovat Scots, was formed by Lord Lovat as a 'sharpshooter' and reconnaissance unit in 1900, and was made up of deer-stalkers, gamekeepers and ghillies from across the Highlands and Islands.

Thanks once more to Erica Munro, as well as to Alison Rae and Andrew Simmons at Birlinn for their sterling editorial work.

My research in South Africa was greatly helped by Anthony Hocking, Arnold van Dyk, Pam McFadden from the Talana Museum, Dennis McDonald, Simon and Cheryl Blackburn, Piet Swart, Johan Loock, Thabo Kruger and Redge Henning. Thank you.

A.M.

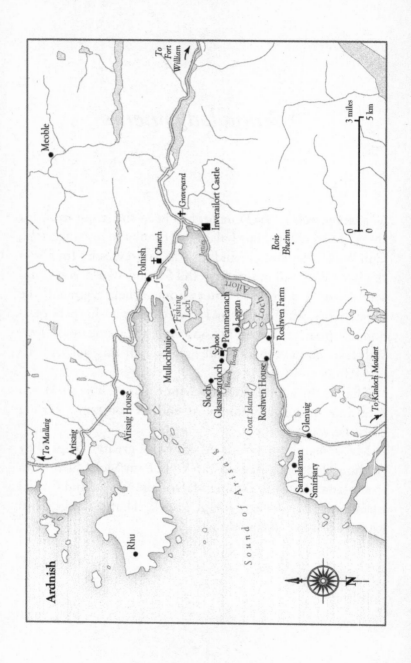

Ardnish

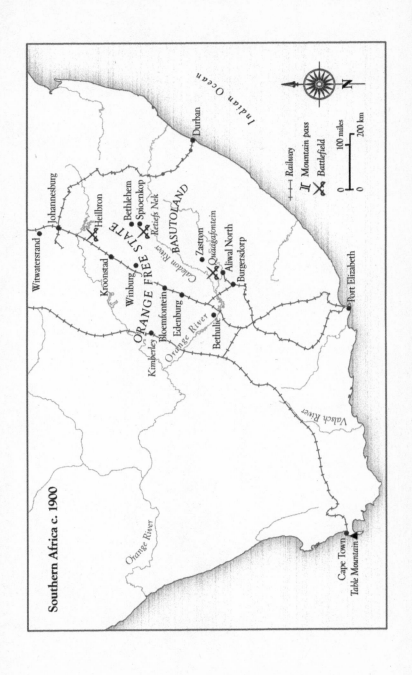

Southern Africa c. 1900

Indian Ocean

Durban

Johannesburg

Witwatersrand

Heilbron

Bethlehem
Spioenkop
Retiefs Nek

ORANGE FREE STATE

BASUTOLAND

Kroonstad

Winburg

Caledon River

Zastron
Quaggafontein
Aliwal North
Burgersdorp

Bloemfontein

Kimberley

Edenburg

Orange River

Bethulie

Port Elizabeth

Orange River

Valsch River

Cape Town
Table Mountain

Railway
Mountain pass
Battlefield

100 miles
200 km

N

Chapter 1

Donald John Gillies, Ardnish, January 1944

I can hear the waves on the shore and the rhythmic drip-drip-drip of water into the bucket under the leak by the fire. The lamp's turned down to save oil and the peat is barely glowing in the hearth. I contemplate life in the silence of the house though my thoughts are often interrupted by terrible bouts of coughing and I'm trembling with a chill. It's pneumonia I'm suffering from. I've known plenty who have had it. A neighbour used to describe it as 'the old man's friend', whisking us away quickly when the time comes.

I have been conscious of my strength ebbing away over the last day or so, but I have kept the thought to myself. My wife Morag is not here, but our great friend Mairi and daughter-in-law Louise are, and they have enough to be worrying about, tending to all the chores around the croft, without the extra worry of this old man. I am fortunate in these two.

Morag headed off to the funeral of her sister in Glasgow several days ago. They weren't close – she'd be the first to admit that – but after some dithering, off she went, taking the train from Lochailort. I was quite well the day she left, and, in any case, Mairi and Louise promised to look after me. Louise went to Arisaig yesterday to send a telegram; my wife should be back any day now.

My hand reaches from beneath the damp blanket to touch the heavy leather bagpipe case which lies empty under the bed. Donald Angus took a lighter army-issue canvas one when he left for the Rockies. The bagpipes were played at the rising of the clans in Glenfinnan when Prince Charles came in 1745 and they have piped men into battle at every war since. They have played at dinners for many of the famous men in the land and at weddings for the most beautiful of brides. My grandson played them at the most famous of all pibroch competitions only recently. My heart swells with pride at the thought. Unless the MacCrimmon family from Dunvegan have an original set, then ours is the most renowned in the Highlands.

My own father, a Cameron Highlander, played them at the Battle of Balaclava in the Crimea as a boy soldier, and my grandfather played them at Waterloo. With the pipers always at the front leading the men into battle, how my ancestors lived to return is a miracle. As I think of piping, my fingers move to a forgotten tune. My grandfather proudly told me when I was a lad that at the Battle of Quatre Bras our men were struggling – half had been killed or injured – but the next morning at Waterloo, piper Kenneth MacKay stepped outside the square and played the ancient pibroch rallying tune '*Cogadh no Sith*'. Our men's backs straightened, their resolve stiffened, and their famous Highland fighting spirit was rejuvenated. By nightfall the great army of Napoleon had been destroyed.

My toe itches, too, as it often does, only there isn't a foot there. I left that in South Africa. I close my eyes and my mind drifts all the way back to my soldiering days . . .

I must have fallen asleep, for when I open my eyes the fire has burned low in the grate and a man is sitting by my bed, looking down at me with kindly eyes.

'Sorry to wake you, Father,' my son says, clasping my hands in his. He isn't wearing his priestly garb, but the crucifix I gave him after his ordination is pinned on his jumper.

I smile, delighted to see him. 'I wasn't asleep, Angus, lad, just dreaming. A happy dream.' But then a thought occurs to me. 'What are you doing here? I thought you were in Edinburgh. Are you on holiday?'

He looks down for a moment as though wondering how to reply.

'I wrote to him.' Louise has entered from outside, carrying peat for the fire.

Angus rises to help her stack the turfs by the hearth and returns to my bedside. 'I came on the nine o'clock train last night and walked down here in the dark. I didn't want to wake you so I slept in Aunt Mairi's house. How are you?'

'Fine,' I say, 'just fine.' Both he and I know that I'm not, of course.

He pulls my blanket up around my shoulders before turning to assist Louise with preparing vegetables for soup. In soft voices they discuss how I'm faring. I hear the odd word from Louise: 'being difficult', 'doctor' and 'medicine'. I chuckle to myself and note with approval how my son is his usual courteous self, asking his sister-in-law about how things are here on the croft and listening intently to her responses.

She's a good woman, Louise, I think for the umpteenth time. Always a kind word on her lips, always helpful and happy to go on errands. She'll stop and have a blether with everyone she meets. Her Gaelic is fluent now, no doubt about it, but I detect a slight Welsh lilt in her voice still.

I vividly remember the day she stepped off the boat at Peanmeanach for the first time. I was standing outside the house, scanning the boatmen's faces, desperately seeking our son, Donald Peter, home from the war with his new wife. But he was not there.

Despite her grief at his death, Louise stayed on and made her home here in Peanmeanach, giving birth to Donald Angus and raising him to be the fine young man he is today. He serves with the Lovat Scouts; first he was in France and Italy, and now he's in Canada. It breaks all of our hearts that my son did not live to see his only child.

I can hear Louise and Father Angus talking about the state of the path, how it has again been washed away at one point. Angus is describing how he had to struggle through the darkness to get here.

There is a rush of icy air as the door swings open and Mairi enters. She's carrying a tin of oatcakes fresh from the stove in her croft next door. 'The wind is swinging to the north east,' she says. 'Snow is coming. How are you feeling, Donald John?'

'All the better for having Angus here,' I reply, summoning my strength to sound as cheerful as I can though my smile is soon followed by a painful coughing fit. Mairi pours me a cup of water from the jug on the table and I sip it gratefully.

Mairi recounts how Angus arrived in the small hours, mud up to his knees where he'd fallen off the track and blood on his face where a branch had swiped him. Angus protests that he had a lamp when he set off, but it went out. He knows the route well enough, but he encountered unexpected rocks here and there, and branches had grown treacherously over some parts of it.

'Some of it has been completely washed away,' Angus says. 'The usual part.' I know the exact point he means: not far west of the railway bridge, where the track crosses the steep hillside. We have often had to rebuild it over the years as the ferocious winter weather always succeeds in eroding our best efforts.

I remember, as a boy, the men of the village meeting to discuss whether a different route could be found, one that could take a cart. These men would meet for a few minutes each morning to discuss their concerns and the jobs that needed to be done. It was Jock Ferguson from St Kilda who got it going. We started calling it a 'parliament', like they did on Hirta.

I recall Donald Angus and Louise's younger brother Owen heading off to fix that bit 'once and for all' when they were lads. They were going to cut some silver birch and embed posts with rails between, then fill it in with stone. I gave them detailed instructions and they did a good job, but that was ten years ago and our wet winters have the ability to destroy everything put there by man. The County Council used to send men to repair the path, but that stopped.

I sigh and shake my head. Life has grown harder and harder here on Ardnish, and I lament for the thousandth time that the loss of my leg has prevented me from being of greater use over the past four decades.

Having no safe pathway to get back and forth will be the last straw for the women. They'll be the only people left behind here in Peanmeanach after I'm gone. They've been dying to move to Arisaig and get a good house and live an easier life, and I know fine that when I'm buried, they'll be out of the house as fast as hares. If Donald Angus doesn't make it home that will be it, the last people on the Ardnish peninsula. Down from a population of two hundred and forty in five clachans in the 1841 Census to none a century later. The MacDonalds, the MacQueens, the Gillies, the Fergusons, the MacDougalls and many others have long gone, mostly to Glasgow, Nova Scotia and Australia. Hands that milked cows, gathered whelks and made hay are now making armaments in the crowded cities, digging coal or in service. Is their life any better now? I wonder.

Chapter 2

Angus eases me gently upright in my bed and sits beside me as I sip some tea and take a mouthful of porridge. 'When it's so wet and horrid like this, do you ever think back to your time in South Africa?' he asks. 'It would be summer there now, wouldn't it? And light, too, in the evening. All that sunshine – you'd be as black as a native.'

I smile and roll my eyes. I've never been brown, as well he knows. I have a permanent milk-white complexion, even in the summer. My arms and face got freckles, which I found embarrassing as a child. I used to have red hair, but what there is of it now is as white as snow.

Angus's surprise visit has raised my spirits and given me a surge of strength. I feel ready to talk. 'My God, Angus,' I begin, 'you couldn't begin to imagine the heat. The sun flayed us alive. On the ship down to Cape Town, on the first day out of St Helena, the younger men sat on the deck without their shirts on. They were in agony that night, burnt scarlet and with enormous blisters. Hardly anyone slept; they just lay moaning and groaning all over the ship. We older soldiers had tried to tell them, but they just wouldn't listen. They only made that mistake once, I can tell you.

'I heard that the Gordon Highlanders were pinned down at Magersfontein all day under fire from the Boer. They were hiding behind any rock they could find, and the backs of their knees between their kilt and gaiters got incredibly badly sunburnt.'

Angus winces. 'A painful spot.'

'There was a plant called aloe, and if you smeared on the juice it made a big difference. We went down with our black Tam o' Shanters, but thankfully within days we were issued with slouch hats – the same as the Boer had – to keep the sun out of our eyes and protect the backs of our necks. And, of course, the Scouts didn't wear kilts, apart from us pipers sometimes, so that helped, too.'

'Did you ever think of staying out there?' Angus asks. 'You could have sent for Mother and us children to join you.'

My heart jolts, and I pause for a few moments before answering with care. After all, Angus will have no idea what my first thought is and I am anxious to be truthful in everything I say. 'Well, yes, son, I did. As did many of us. In fact, thirty-nine Lovat Scouts signed on as members of the Transvaal police and remained out there. Baden-Powell was recruiting, and I imagine many of them didn't have much to come back to. Dugald MacDonald from Bohuntin stayed out. He was a good friend of mine, and something of a hero out there. You wouldn't have come across him, I don't suppose? He came here for a visit once, many years ago.'

Angus shakes his head.

The memories relax me as I warm to my subject. 'Imagine,' I continue, 'if you were from Brae Roy, you were twenty-four and the third son, with no croft or livelihood to speak of, and no girl to come back for. The land out there is beautiful – rich dark-red soil, knee-deep grass in summer – and the cattle and sheep are twice the size of ours. You could get a well-paid job in the police, that came with a house. I was tempted. But my heart is here, in Ardnish, and I had the family to return to . . . and of course after the massacre I wasn't about to get a job with a missing leg, was I? No, it was retirement for me, aged just forty-five, and an invalid's pension.'

We fall silent. I do have another tale to tell, but I vow my son will not hear it. Not a word of it has passed my lips since the day it came to an end. Though once, many years ago, when I was at the auction mart at the Garrison, I was approached by John MacDonald the Boss, from the Volunteer Arms, who asked what the real story was about me in South Africa. I angrily told him to mind his own business and hold his tongue, before turning my back on him. Even my close friend Colonel Willie never mentioned it after the war though he knew the truth better than anyone. We never discussed it despite spending many hours fishing together on the lochan here above the village.

Angus must have seen me drift off into my own thoughts. He makes to move away. 'I'll let you rest now,' he says.

'Don't go,' I say. 'I'm enjoying talking to you.'

He smiles and sits back down on the edge of the box bed. 'If you're sure you've got the strength.'

'With the summer came the storms. It was so hot you would burn your hand picking up an ammunition box at midday. Then, sure as eggs are eggs, in mid-afternoon the sky would blacken dark as night, you would hear the thunder in the distance, and the wind would blow dust in all directions. The horses' ears would go back and they'd tug on their ropes, and within half an hour all hell would break loose. There would be a crack of lightning so vivid it would hurt your eyes, and sometimes the thunder was so loud no artillery or passing train could compare. The noise of it! And then came the rain. Like a hundred buckets of water being poured over you all at once.'

I glance at Angus to see if he's imagining the maelstrom. 'It's so difficult to describe,' I say. 'No matter how dramatic I try to make it sound I feel as though I cannot do it justice. You have to experience an African storm to understand its power. Even the worst storms here come nowhere close.'

Angus widens his eyes. 'As if you didn't have enough to contend with out there!'

'The thing is, within the hour it would all be back to normal. The puddles evaporated in minutes in the evening sun and it would become ten degrees cooler.

'So, what would happen during the summer months is that when we were out on patrol, we would ready our horses and set off at first light, at five or even earlier in the morning. It was warm by eight and unbearable by eleven. We would pitch our tents and get fires going for a brew and some food, then we would take cover before the inevitable storm hit. Mind you, sometimes we had no choice but to ride through it. At times like those the horses were a hell of a job to hang on to. They were terrified of the storms and wanted to bolt.

'You might cross a riverbed in the morning with only a trickle of water but by nightfall you'd be hanging onto your horse's mane as it struggled to swim through the current. If you were fording a river and saw lightning miles away upstream, you had to be sure to get over the *spruit* – that was what they called a creek – before a torrent of water came along. More than a few men were killed that way.

'Winter was another thing altogether. Much cooler of course, but seldom cold during the day, and little rain. The grass became short and brown. On the border with Basutoland, up at six thousand feet, we occasionally got snow, but it was rare.'

The memories are flooding into my mind, but I'm becoming weary. I look at my son, longing to tell him more, but I'll do so later. 'Never mind my old memories. Tell me what you've been up to, and what news do you have of the Camerons?' I'm always interested to hear about my old regiment, although it will be my contemporaries' grandsons serving in it now – quite a thought. Angus has been the regiment chaplain for two years and seems to know exactly what they're up to.

'The regiment has just arrived in Italy, Father. I received a letter from a friend in the Cavalry, Denzil Skinner, and read it on the train from Glasgow. He's in a brigade that is amassing in Taranto, ready for a push up the east coast to Puglia. He says that the war is nearly won, but there is some stiff fighting ahead of them. Wait, I have it here.'

He fetches his bag and rifles through it, talking as he searches. 'It paints such a vivid image; you'll enjoy it.' He finds the letter, then returns to my side and begins to read a segment. ' "We heard, although we could scarcely believe it, the skirl of pipes. There, in the brilliant sunshine, marching down the centre of the road from the escarpment, came a long column of men, almost a thousand. The traffic was brought to a standstill or forced onto the verges. A strange, awed murmur went up: 'The Camerons!' In columns of threes they marched with a swing to the tune of their pipers: 'The March of The Cameron Men'. Each company was led by its company commander, just as though they were on parade. It was a supremely moving sight, although some of us could only see it hazily through our tears."'

I confess I am nearly in tears myself.

'The Camerons have had a terrible war, Father,' Angus murmurs. 'Enormous losses at Dunkirk and again at Tobruk, but even so, they're still the most sought-after regiment for recruits . . .'

We both sit in silence, alone with our thoughts of these fine kilted men, whose fathers, grandfathers and great-grandfathers, too, would have marched with pride in their Cameron of Erracht tartan.

'Oh, and there was one odd occasion I must tell you about,' he says. 'I was at the cathedral in Edinburgh just recently when I was given a message that a Canadian soldier wanted to see me. We had a cup of tea and a blether, and at the end of it I still wasn't entirely sure why he was there. Calum Beaton was his name, and he had the Gaelic.

'It was as if he was fishing for information. He told me he was not long married to a girl called Morag and lived in Cape Breton. He kept asking about my family. It was really quite strange.'

My son is looking at me intently as if he wants me to acknowledge the name. Should it mean something to me? 'I'm sorry,' I reply, 'but I don't understand. Did this man know our Sheena?'

'He didn't say,' Angus replies. 'The whole encounter was odd.'

After breakfast, and with everyone settled around the warmth of the stove, I call out to Angus. He comes over and sits by my bed. I can see the concern on his face.

'I want to say my last confession,' I say, avoiding his eyes. My voice is weak, but I feel, suddenly, strong.

He smiles, reaches across and takes my hand. 'I will hear it, and gladly. It's so good that I'm here.'

I pause awkwardly. Angus, no doubt, thinks my confession will be the usual things: cursing, unkind thoughts and so on. After all, what else could this old man have to confess?

'No, son. Please ask Canon MacNeil from Arisaig to come.'

We are both silent for a moment, embarrassed.

'But why?' There is a note of hurt in my son's voice, which pains me.

'Angus,' I whisper, 'you are a fine priest. But you are also my son. And it is as my son that I want you by my side today.'

'Of course. I'm sorry,' he replies.

But Mairi is harder to convince. 'What nonsense, Donald John,' she cries. 'You have a perfectly good priest here on the spot and you want to waste Canon MacNeil's time – and asking him to come in this weather, too!'

I can't argue with Mairi's logic but fortunately Louise comes to my aid. 'I'll go and get him right away,' she announces. 'If he's at St Mary's he'll hopefully come immediately. He'll have to stay overnight, of course.'

'Watch out for the weather, yourself,' I say as Louise puts on her coat and looks for a stick. Angus gives her the ration book and a list of messages. Mairi quickly prepares a piece to keep her going.

'I'll wear your Tam o' Shanter if that's all right with you, Donald John?' Louise calls over to me. She likes to wear it. I suspect it reminds her of Donald Peter. That old family black-and-white Lovat Scout bonnet has been used by her more than by myself these past years.

It's a long way for Canon MacNeil to come from Arisaig. It will take half a day each way on his pony, and that's not even taking into account the difficulties he may encounter with the weather and with parts of the footpath being washed away. I fear he might struggle to get his pony along it at all and he may be forced to come on foot.

Mairi has gone back to her house next door, to the peace of her loom, and my son has gone for a walk over to Laggan along the shore. And so I am left alone with my troubled thoughts, and begin to compose my confession in my mind.

Chapter 3

Donald John, January 1900

Morag and I had been married for twenty-three years and our children were growing up fast. The older two were ready to leave home, and only little Donald Peter still went to school. Sheena was away a lot, in service at Roshven House during the summer when the Blackburns had guests and helping around the village. She'd find any excuse to go to a ceilidh in Arisaig or further afield, and often stayed away for a few days at a time. She had itchy feet, that was for sure. Her younger brother, Angus, was seventeen, three years her junior, fit and strong.

Morag often spoke to him about what he might do with his life. She would urge him to leave Lochaber, to seek an easier life than one scratching a living from this hard ground. He was like me though, with an emotional tie to the Highlands. I knew it would take a greater calling than money to drag him away. I once asked him if he would join the army and see the world like I did myself at his age, but he just shook his head. I was hardly surprised; he'd be the last person to stab someone with a bayonet. He wouldn't hurt a fly, he was so gentle a man. That said, he wouldn't be pushed around. If I wanted him to fix a gate or a bridge or some such task, he would do it in his own sweet time. There were often angry words between us because of it.

Donald Peter, my wee man, was twelve. He was always at my side, holding a hammer or a piece of wood, keen to get involved with some joinery work. Not so wee, in truth; he was almost my height and very funny. We always had a laugh as we worked together. He was doing very well at school, spoke English fluently, and his teacher, Mr Erskine, remarked that there wasn't much more Latin he could teach him, such was his rare gift for languages.

As a young man, I had made good money in the army; later, the constant renovations at Roshven House kept me fully employed. There were always buildings being added. First, the east wing, then both east and west gate lodges, and later, the stables they referred to as the Square. I was the joiner there, and all the windows, doors and shutters were made by me and a couple of lads from Glenuig. My wages kept us well fed, and we were able to buy some decent furniture and a good pony. I used to think to myself that we must be the most comfortably-off family on Ardnish. The last few years had been tougher though. The previous winter, a whole three months had gone by without a penny of income coming into the family. There was plenty of unpaid work, repairing nets or fixing fishing boats when a wooden stave caved in, and instead of seeking employment all the time I taught myself to make baskets out of hazel and willow. But as I wove, Morag would sweep briskly around me in the house, making me feel that I wasn't really working. She said more than once that basketmaking was a tinker's job. But in the spring, I took a dozen of my baskets down to Helensburgh on the puffer which was delivering supplies. It was said to be the richest town in Britain, and I thought I might be able to sell the baskets there. I walked around for two days trying my hardest to get a good price, and when I eventually came back with a couple of guineas, Morag dismissed my efforts, telling me that I'd sold them too cheap and the shopkeeper would make three times that. She told me that the next time I should go around the big mansions that were being built around the town and charm the ladies. I often felt I could do nothing right.

Morag was hard on me. I felt I was under her feet all the time and failing her – a disappointment. Our past intimacies and shared laughter were things of the past. When she came in at dusk from her day's work, she would put the kettle on, barely acknowledging me in the corner where I'd be squinting in the dim light of the kerosene lamp, trying to mend a shoe or strip bark off willow. She was always busy with the animals or helping the older people in the village, and both of us were worried sick about feeding the family over the coming winter.

I remember eyeing up the two beautiful Orkney chairs I'd bought her in Glasgow for our tenth wedding anniversary on my way home on leave from the army, and wondering how she'd react if I told her I'd found myself wondering how much we'd be able to sell them for now. She had coveted chairs like these since she was a girl and I remember her excitement when she first set eyes on them. She had thrown her arms around me and told me I was the best husband in the world that day. I know if I took them off to sell, I'd become the worst. But things were so bad I felt I had few other options.

During the summer I had been kept busy rebuilding an internal wall at the west end of Roshven House – the damp was making it uninhabitable – and making two new windows. But as the owners, Professor and Mrs Blackburn, grew older, construction work began to tail off. I had day work with the ponies when the Astley-Nicholsons of Arisaig House came stalking on Ardnish, but gradually we went from being comfortably off to poor. Morag picked whelks, milked the cow, and looked after the few sheep on Ardnish as well as her three weeks of lambing at Borrodale but that was it as far as income went.

It was late August that year when I got word that men were needed for a big cattle drive from Glenelg down to Falkirk. We were told we would be away for three months. The money wasn't good, and the man leading the drove was John Mackenzie, a Wester Ross man whom both Morag and I had met before. He was a brute of a man with a terrible temper and was rumoured to have once beaten a man to death.

Morag and I spoke about it late into the night. By God, we needed the money and this would see us through the winter, but it would be miserable for me sleeping out in the winter's rain with just a sodden wool blanket, never mind putting up with the inevitable abuse from Mackenzie. However, I made up my mind to go. I needed to get away and I thought maybe this would restore my wife's belief in me.

But Morag wasn't having it. She said I was being stubborn and I would die my death of cold and it just wasn't worth it. It turned into a heated argument, with words that would haunt us later and young Donald John clinging to her, crying at us to stop shouting. I eventually conceded and agreed not to go, and later was to be grateful that Morag had forced me to overcome my pride and stay in Peanmeanach.

We had rarely argued in years gone by, but the lack of money was dispiriting and Morag worked so hard she was always exhausted and irritable. Gone were the days of putting my arm around her as we sat by the fire talking about our life or sneaking off to bed together when the children were at school. Years before, when I came back on army leave from Egypt each summer for six weeks, we would walk along the coastline of the Ardnish peninsula with a picnic. I'd spread out my plaid and we would make love in the heather. Those were the days.

Stalking with the Arisaig House guests always resulted in good tips and was enjoyable work, even though on Ardnish it would only be three or four days a year, in October. One of the gardeners would come across the week before and give me instructions. Morag would tidy me up, insisting I shaved and dressed in the tweed jacket and plus fours which Mairi had made for me. I relished those days away, the fresh air in my lungs, the challenge of man against beast and the conversation with men who lived completely different lives from myself. On those days I would be guilt-ily delighted that there would be no hoeing of the kale patch or picking stones from the big field, my least favour-ite chores.

I was only an occasional stalker, but when the rut was at its peak and there were a couple of parties already out elsewhere on the estate I would get my chance. I fancied myself at it, and more often than not we'd have a good stag by the end of the day.

I'd go to meet the laird, Sir Arthur Astley-Nicholson, and his guest by Lochan Dubh at nine in the morning. The previous day I'd have spied the ground and located a suitable stag or two. I was provided with a pony and a ghillie to carry the beast back to the larder. Sir Arthur would become enraged if the stalk was ruined by any passers-by, and so, before the big day I would spread the word that people should stay in their clachans. Woe betide anyone who scared off the deer.

I remember one hot summer's afternoon in particular. The laird was out with a Member of Parliament as his guest when a man from Glasgow wandered up with a fishing rod. We intercepted him and told him of our stalking plans. He replied aggressively that he didn't care what our plans were; he was off fishing and would do just as he wanted, where he wanted and he didn't care if he ruined our day or not.

We went back and forth and up and down, covering every inch of the peninsula, and didn't encounter a stag all day. Sir Arthur had been keen to show his guest some good sport and as we turned for home he furiously blamed the fruitless day on the belligerent angler.

On the way back, as we passed along the path to the west of Loch Doir a'Ghearrain we caught a glimpse of the man, swimming naked. With great glee, the laird and the MP crept up, took the man's clothing and boots, and we all retired to a safe spot to watch what happened next. The fisherman emerged from the loch and hunted and hunted for his clothes. Then, as he realised what had happened he began shouting obscenities, furiously waving his fists in the air. It was early evening and there wasn't a breath of wind in the air – just when the midges were at their most voracious. We all thought this a well-deserved prank and walked off half a mile before the laird, waving off midges himself, relented and left the man's clothing on the path.

I heard later from Mrs McCallum at Lochailort Inn that the man had been the most unpleasant guest and she had been delighted to hear of his mishap and subsequent early departure from the area.

I had very much hoped to be taken on by Sir Arthur as a full-time stalker but the role was keenly sought after. In any event, the two men who were already in post weren't so old as myself, and despite my many hints, Sir Arthur wasn't tempted to have a third man down at the south end of the estate. So, in the absence of regular work anywhere, I had to make do with whatever occasional employment came my way. But things had become desperate and I feared for our very survival.

Chapter 4

On New Year's Day in 1900, I had to take old Donald MacVarish, who had suffered a badly broken arm, to hospital in Fort William. After leaving him to be treated, I met my good friend Captain Willie MacDonald in the High Street. He told me he was seeing his mother, I told him of my errand, and we decided to toast in the new century in the Volunteer Arms with a tot of his family's Long John whisky.

'It's a bad day to be away from the peninsula,' I joked, 'but I'm sure my liver will benefit!'

Although a decade younger than myself, we'd got on well ever since I'd been a corporal and him a subaltern in the Camerons in 1890. A young officer, however well born, knows little, and I was a seasoned soldier from my years in North Africa. My job was to be his batman, his personal servant. I looked after his horse and protected him in battle. We built a professional relationship but quickly forged a deep personal bond through our shared love of the people and the way of life in the West Highlands.

With our drams in our hands, Captain Willie and I had a long talk about my family and how they were doing. He knew them well, especially my youngest, for whom he had

a soft spot. 'Is he keeping at the piping?' he enquired
eagerly. Donald Peter's progress with his piping was always
an early question of his. I told him that Donald MacDonald
in the village was tutoring him now, as well as MacDougall,
who was concentrating on his pibroch. He was incredibly
fortunate to have two such remarkable pipers nearby.
Captain Willie knew of both and nodded approvingly. I
told him proudly about Donald Peter's ability with
languages and how pleased the teacher was with him.

'And how is Morag?' he asked.

I found myself avoiding his eyes as I replied, 'She's well,
thank you for asking. Keeping busy as always.'

'She must come over to Blarour and compete in the
sheep dog trials this year.' He smiled. 'Hosting that event
on the farm is my highlight of the year, and I know Morag
would give the men a good run for their money!'

I promised I would try to persuade her though I knew it
wouldn't be difficult. Morag was a natural with her dog at
the sheep. I confided in him my concerns about Angus and
what he might do now he was finished school. Although
my son was kind and generous, a powerful runner and the
strongest young man I knew, none of that would feed a
family.

'I'd take him on at the distillery, you know I would, but
I'm afraid we're laying men off at the moment. But tell him
we can always find a room for him with my mother at
Invernevis if he wants to come and work in town for a
while.'

I nodded my gratitude and enquired after his mother.

'Doughty,' he replied after a moment's hesitation.
'Always busy . . .' He drained his glass.

I could see he was troubled but knew better than to press him on family issues. Seeking a more neutral topic, I changed tack. 'And how are your distilleries faring? Your older brother Jack is in charge nowadays, is he not?'

'Not well, I'm afraid,' came the reply. 'It's not that he's doing a bad job, it's the whole industry that's suffering.'

'That's a pity, what with Long John being the biggest employer in the area.'

'Over two hundred and thirty men . . .' the captain sighed, before changing the subject. 'And how are things at Ardnish? Still working at Roshven House?'

I could sense the deflection and answered his question. 'Times are hard, as you can imagine. Money is tight. The Blackburns have been good employers since I left the Camerons, but the building works are finished and the work has dried up.' I could feel my face reddening as I went on. 'I've resorted to weaving baskets and making creels to bring in a bit of money.'

He raised his eyebrows at that, clearly of the same opinion as Morag that this wasn't a real man's job.

'It may be that we'll have to go to Glasgow or emigrate to Nova Scotia. It seemed unthinkable to me until recently, but I worry constantly, about Donald Peter in particular. Some days we have only boiled nettle soup and oatcakes to eat.'

Captain Willie cleared his throat and looked at me. 'Goodness, man, that sounds grim. You know, I think I might be able help.'

I was flustered. 'No! Please, don't worry. We're fine. There are many more in a worse position than us. I really wasn't asking for help. I shouldn't have mentioned it.'

He smiled. 'Luckily, I think I have a fine opportunity for the two of us. I had you in mind anyway and was planning to come and find you at Peanmeanach.' He summoned the barman and, furnished with another dram, laid out the opportunity. 'Lord Simon Lovat is raising a regiment to go and fight the Boer in South Africa,' he said. 'I've been asked to join as adjutant. I would like you to come, too, to look after me. We are to be the scouting regiment of the army, made up of ghillies and stalkers. We need to bring our ponies, and we'll be paid well to bring them, plus extra money if we bring a telescope. A few of the lairds are donating them. I'm sure Astley-Nicholson will donate a couple if I ask him. The pay is not tremendous for a private, but we'll get you made up to a corporal as soon as we can – if you behave yourself,' he added with a wink.

The pay he quoted certainly got my attention. The daily rate would take me a week to amass here, collecting whelks or working for the Astley-Nicholsons. It wasn't just the money though. I suddenly realised I could do with getting away from the village and from Morag, who was without doubt growing increasingly disappointed in me. I craved adult male company, excitement and a challenge. The winter stretched long ahead of us, another four months of long nights, damp and cold. Africa sounded very tempting indeed.

I didn't mention these thoughts to the captain. 'I'm forty-four now,' I told him, 'and hardly a horseman either. But I could certainly do with the money now that there's no work around Ardnish. If you'll have me, I'll come.'

He made me promise not to mention my age and told me to write on the paperwork that I was thirty-eight – forty was the maximum age for anyone to serve. We were to meet in Fort William, in Cameron Square, on the four-teenth of the month, at ten in the morning, dressed in tweeds and ready to go. A dozen men from Lochaber would also be there. Meanwhile, he would get me signed up. A letter confirming the details would follow, to which I needed to reply with the information they needed. When they received that, I was promised, my pay would start.

The captain's brother, Jack, had offered to host a big send-off ceilidh at the Invernevis distillery the night before, and all our families were invited to come along. I was certain that Morag wouldn't come, but Sheena almost certainly would. In any event, the prospect of fine food and endless whisky would ensure a packed room.

As I rode my pony the thirty miles back home, I had plenty of time to consider things. Morag would be furious. I was too old. I'd get killed or injured, and what use would I be to her then? But on the other hand, we had no money and 'taking the King's shilling' was a long tradition in the West Highlands when families were hungry.

Perhaps deep down she wouldn't mind, I tried to persuade myself. I suspected, with a heavy heart, that she needed a break from me, too. I recalled how when we were first married she had coped well when I was on duty abroad. But now the village community was more fragile; with the emigrations there were fewer young folk around and more to do. And she had the children to worry about. What lay in store for them?

Donald Peter was waiting for me when I got home that evening, smiling as always. 'I've been playing the pipes, Father,' he said. 'I've nearly got "The Braes Of Castle Grant" off by heart.'

I patted him on the back. 'Go out and find Sandy,' I said gently. 'I need to have a word with your mother.'

'How is old Donald's arm?' Morag asked straight away. 'Will they be able to mend it at his age?' We both knew it mattered desperately, for if the doctor couldn't fix it, then digging in the fields or picking whelks would be impossible and then what would he and his older sister live on? Others in the village would give them food but they were proud people.

'It will be fine,' I reassured her. 'He needs to stay in the Fort for a couple of weeks. But that's not why I sent DP off to play.' I paused. 'Morag, I'm off to fight in South Africa.'

Morag regarded me in silence. I ploughed on. 'I met Captain Willie MacDonald in the High Street and he told me Lord Lovat's raising a new regiment.'

Morag had a high opinion of the Long John MacDonalds, and Lord Lovat owned an estate in Morar, so I hoped the familiarity would appease her a bit. 'I'll be paid a shilling a day. I leave in a fortnight.'

'Well, you can't go, Donald John! You just can't! What about your family? You're needed here. We need you to plant the seed in the spring, help with the boats, help raise Angus and Donald Peter – you know they're at a sensitive stage in their lives.' She sank into the chair by the stove and gave in to tears.

I laid my hand on her shoulder and tried to comfort her as best I could under the onslaught of sobbing. 'But, Morag,' I pleaded, 'you know how desperately we need the money. It's either I go to Africa for maybe a year and make enough to keep us for five – which means DP can stay at the school here – or we move to Glasgow and I try to get a job in the shipyards.'

She knew it would break my heart to leave Peanmeanach for ever. We'd had this discussion many times over the last couple of years. We both wanted Donald Peter to continue attending the school at Feorlindhu. He was doing so well, and it had given such a great education to Angus and Sheena.

'And what about me?' she cried. 'You can't just walk out on me! I need you. I may as well be widowed if you go to Africa. You might not come home, Donald John. What if you never come back?'

I was taken aback by this. It hadn't seemed that she had needed me at all over the last few years. I had often felt little more than a nuisance to her. But I held my tongue.

'You're just a selfish man, selfish!' she shouted, before storming out of the house and slamming the door behind her.

I knew I wouldn't see her for hours. She'd head out into the hills with her sheepdog and not return until well after dark. Perhaps she would check on the sheep, or visit Mairi next door to rage about me, or just sit by the shore staring out to sea. I knew better than to go after her.

With the house to myself, I sat and brooded at the fireplace, listlessly prodding the peat embers with the poker. Although sorry to have upset Morag, I knew that I was frustrated and bored. I had been offered a real lifeline. There wasn't much left of my life when I would be strong and fit enough to do something significant, and this seemed to me to be my last chance. Yes, I was being selfish, but the opportunity was just too good to miss. I'd hopefully be back in a year, there would be money, those beautiful Orkney chairs would still be here, and perhaps our marriage would be rekindled – all the stronger for my temporary absence. My leaving would also give Angus a bit more responsibility on the peninsula. He would flourish, of that I was certain. Young Angus was very handy to have around the place, but because we were clashing more and more often, there was often an uncomfortable atmosphere. I think we knew that either he or I would have to go away for a while. My absence would give him space to decide on his future. Sheena wouldn't be affected so much; if she wasn't at work, she was over at Smirisary with her man, Colin Angus, these days. He would row over to pick her up in his wee boat, a good four hours there and back. I had fewer fears for her future.

I had been in bed a while when Morag finally came back in. 'Are you awake?' she said softly. 'We need to talk more about this.'

She had obviously been doing a lot of thinking and she laid out her objections in a level voice with only occasional bursts of anger and tears. There was more about the jobs that needed doing around the place, more about the children and how could I do this to them, more about the uncertainty of my return. I remonstrated weakly and gently, knowing the battle was won. We both knew I was off.

Lying in our small bed, Morag and I talked on, late into the night. 'Men love the excitement and camaraderie of soldiering,' she said sadly. 'Men, always men, in the cities think nothing of sending other people's children off to die in vain. Then, after countless thousands of casualties a truce is called and some soldiers eventually make it home – but they're different, broken men from when they left.

The whole thing is absurd! And it's us, the families, who bear the cost!'

The next evening, the children were all at home and I broke the news to them. Morag held her tongue but they knew her views on the matter. After they got over the shock there was even some excitement, and a discussion about the animals I would see: lions and elephants, maybe? Angus, predictably, doubted how much use I would be in battle. However, by the end of the evening the children seemed to have fully accepted my departure, which was a relief for me and, I think, for Morag, too. I suggested that I might take our pony with me but the outcry that greeted this meant I quickly backed down. I knew I would make more money by bringing one with me, and so Morag eventually said that Mairi would sell me one of hers, but it would be at a high price.

Sheena and Angus were both heading over to Glenuig the next day, but they promised they would be back to see me off. The two of them had recently moved into Alistair Ruadh's house at the end of the row; he and his wife had emigrated to Cape Breton in the autumn, following their son who had gone out two years before and now sent money for their passage. Before they went, they had said that our two older ones could look after their house in Peanmeanach in case things didn't work out in Canada. Sheena and Angus had jumped at the chance.

When I woke the next morning, I could see the weak winter sun touching the top of Roshven Hill through the window. My hand reached out for Morag's as it always did, but today she rolled over, away from me. Her collie came out from under the bed to greet me instead.

It was not until the tea was made and porridge on the table that Morag finally spoke. 'You are not considering us, Donald John. You are off for a thrill, to get away from the winter. You know fine all your chores will become mine. I'll be slaving away here in your beloved Ardnish looking after your people, waiting for a man who might not come back. You do know men die at war, don't you?'

I couldn't muster a word in my defence. Instead, I reached out once more for her hand, but she pulled it away. I had always seen Morag as a strong, pragmatic woman and was surprised she was taking my departure so badly. But at the same time, I felt some pleasure that she seemed to care so much.

'*Mo ghràidh*,' I said after a time, 'when I get back, so many of our troubles will have gone. With all the money I'll get, buying kerosene for the lamps or paint for the windows and the boat won't be a worry any more! And I'm nearing fifty, I need one last adventure. Please, Morag, can't you understand?'

'Angus is itching to be away,' she said simply, as if she hadn't heard a word I'd said.

'I'll have a word with him – tell him he's the man of the house now.'

The next day the two of us sat awkwardly at the table, sipping our tea. I felt wretched. I wished she would just take my hands, tell me that she loved me, urge me to hurry back to her, tell me that she would be waiting, that she would write often. That she understood. But there was only bitter silence.

Her chair scraped back as she headed out to milk the cow, her collie, as always, trotting at her heel. 'Bring the peat in. The drier fads are behind the byre,' she added unnecessarily as the door slammed behind her.

The following week passed at a snail's pace. I worked as hard as I could to make things easier for Morag, bringing down a couple of tons of peat from the area called the moss for our house and for a couple of the older people in the village. I fixed the leak in the roof that had been a problem for months and I put shoes on Mairi's pony. She'd never been shod before so that was a palaver. The evenings were fine while the youngsters were around; Morag wasn't hostile to me, just indifferent. I felt more like a cousin than her husband.

As the day of my leaving drew closer I was keen to hug her, kiss her, make love to her. I wanted us to part with a shared intimacy which we could both remember. On the eve of my departure the opportunity finally arose. There was no one around and the rain was teeming down outside. 'Darling,' I ventured. I was sitting on the chair, both hands outstretched towards her. 'Please?' I was beseeching her to come to me. Her eyes locked onto mine for a moment, and then she rose to her feet. She gathered up her tweed coat and turned toward the door. 'I need to go over to Laggan,' she said. 'Don't wait up. You'll need your strength for your travels in the morning.'

When I finally rode off the next morning, I was desperate to go. I went around the houses and shook hands with everyone as they wished me good luck and a safe return. I held Morag in my arms as she cried, but she couldn't bring herself to embrace me.

Donald Peter ran alongside my pony until we got to the hill above the big field overlooking the bay. He clung to my leg. 'Come back, Father! We'll die if you don't!' he pleaded. I shooed him off home so he wouldn't see me blubbing like a bairn.

I could see the peat smoke billowing from the houses that were still inhabited, the thatch falling in upon those that were not, the white waves crashing onto the sandy beach that glinted in the winter sun, and Roshven Hill and An Stac deep in snow at their summits. I drank it all in to store in my memory. Then, I turned the pony towards the village one last time and saw my family and friends waving handkerchiefs, still shouting their goodbyes.

But all I could hear was the wind.

Chapter 5

When I reached Fort William, the recruits were lined up in Cameron Square. Seventeen of us were from the Lochaber Contingent; all were mounted. Sergeant Cameron tutted as he tried to make us look like soldiers rather than scruffy estate stalkers all set for a day on the hill. There was a multitude of tweeds: Achnacarry, Meoble, Inverlochy Castle, Mamore and myself wearing the distinctive Arisaig orange tweed woven by Mairi. I played the pipes, worrying all the while that my pony would move off. There was a throng of well-wishers clustered around us and a party atmosphere as we clattered down the road towards Inverness and then on to Beauly.

As we proceeded, we were joined by other recruits. Two Macdonald Knoydart men, then a Loch Quoich stalker with Mr Ellice, the Grant twins from Loch Hourn and more from Glenelg way all joined at Invergarry. By the time we arrived in Beauly there were over forty of us.

At Beauly we were billeted for a month in the stables, the officers in Beaufort Castle. It was incredibly cold, with a foot of snow on the ground. At least half the men had served in the army before; all could shoot and use telescopes but many had no idea how to ride. Our commanding officer, Major Murray of the Cameron Highlanders, was at his wits' end trying to instil discipline. He and Lord Lovat had serious concerns about how the generals would view us against the smart cavalry and guards' regiments. Even Captain MacDonald was given a dressing down for calling me Donald John rather than Gillies. But just before we departed, our uniforms arrived and we finally resembled a fighting unit.

After our month's training, to the tune of '*Morair Sim*', six of us pipers proudly led the battalion down Beauly High Street. The street was packed with people waving Union Jacks and press photographers jostling for the best positions. Our Highland ponies were small and shaggy with long manes which reached below their necks, and some of the taller men's feet were almost trailing on the ground. One of the companies was mounted, the other infantry, although by the time we arrived in Cape Town we were all given horses. We were the main story in every paper in the Highlands, including the *Inverness Courier*, with my face proudly leading the pipers as we bade our leave in Inverness. The accompanying article was stirring:

A CHEERING FAREWELL

Animated scenes were seen at Station Square, Inverness, yesterday, in connection with the departure of Lord Lovat and his regiment of the Highlands' finest men to South Africa. Wives, sweethearts, mothers and children were all there to bid them farewell, but in their goodbyes was a note of absolute confidence, even of lightness. These happy warriors looked remarkably fit; as they boarded, their laughter and good-natured chaff suggested a homecoming party rather than a farewell. As the train pulled out, many of the men were singing a merry song as they waved hats and handkerchiefs out of the window.

We travelled in different ships out to Cape Town. Two Company set sail from Glasgow on the *Tintagel Castle*. I was in First Company, and we went off to Southampton where we were billeted in several inns throughout the city. The men grew rowdy with the excitement of it all; on one occasion, I and three others played the pipes in the main street in the middle of the night. The locals weren't too happy about the noise but the two policemen who came to tell us off were Scottish and let us play on.

There was a Glasgow man in the inn where I was staying, and I got talking to him over a beer. He owned a business called A. & J. Main and was on his way to South Africa to try to win the army contract for corrugated iron sheeting. There was a plan to build blockhouses, connected by barbed-wire fences, across the country. If he succeeded, he would become very wealthy, he hoped. His business made ready-to-erect corrugated iron churches – known as 'tin tabernacles' – which were sold all over the world. He offered me a job if I ever wanted one and I told him that after the war I might well take him up on it.

Before we set sail on the *Glengyle* from Great Britain, we heard that there had already been three disastrous battles. At the battle of Magersfontein, the Highland brigade alone had suffered seven hundred casualties, and our garrisons at Ladysmith and Kimberley were under siege. Until then it had been considered, as one newspaper put it, 'an easy war ... go out there, trounce the Dutch farmers and home for tea'. All of a sudden it was real. We began to train harder and every practice bayonet thrust felt as if there was a real Boer as the target.

It was rough at sea for us, bitterly cold for the first week, then later too hot as we passed down the African coast. A lot of our time was spent looking after the horses, mucking them out and feeding them. Several got a bad infection called pink eye, and some perished. Heaving the carcasses up and over the side was a big job. During storms, we'd be with them the whole time. Their tails would be up, their ears laid flat and their eyes wide with fear as they struggled to keep upright. A close affinity grew between us and our horses.

After initial complaints, the two thousand men on board soon became accustomed to their hammocks, and we especially enjoyed watching shoals of flying fish, some of which flopped onto the decks. We had constant fitness training, target practice using bottles off the stern, and we played cards long into the night. We sharpened our bayonets, were taught hand-to-hand combat and practised crawling long distances on the hard deck.

Lieutenant Kenny Macdonald was the entertainment officer and he organised inter-regimental competitions between the South Staffords, Hampshire Engineers, Prince Alberts and us. Each of them had about seven hundred men, and although we had only a hundred we acquitted ourselves. There were wheelbarrow races, tugs of war (which we won) plus men balancing on a spar, wielding stuffed canvas sail-bags at their opponents. Those with horse-riding experience were always the best at balancing.

It felt like a holiday at times. It was non-stop action and there was not a second to get bored.

Before we left Glasgow for Southampton, one of the distilleries had donated cases of whisky for the men, and each Friday evening Captain MacDonald would issue a bottle to be shared among eight men – a popular gesture. On those same nights there would be a ceilidh, and the Scouts would lay on a show for the ship's company. Gaelic songs, a Skye man with the most wonderful voice, four of us pipers doing a sword dance in our kilts, and officers dancing a Regimental foursome.

As we finally approached land, the decks were packed with men all desperate to see the sights. The navy ratings were begging us all not to stand on one side at the same time, as the ship began to tilt over with the weight. Cape Town harbour was a remarkable sight for us Highland lads. I counted twenty-three ships in the bay, including three hospital ships. There was a tented city as far as the eye could see. Artillery practice was taking place; you could hear the shelling and see a blanket of smoke over towards Table Mountain. A brass band on the pier welcomed the disembarking soldiers, and the horses were led off to their lines. We encountered all sorts of regimental names no one had heard of, such as the Royal Dublin Fusiliers, Thorneycroft's Mounted Infantry and Paget's Horse, as well as many thousands of foreign soldiers: Canadians, Australians, Indian Sikhs. A team of oxen were dragging an enormous gun away from the docks. Our eyes were out on stalks. The entire might of the Imperial Army was massing here to take on only sixty thousand Boer – surely it couldn't be too difficult?

I was grateful to have a good friend, a man from Lochielside called Donald Cameron. Known as Cammy, he was one of the older men like myself, and had been in the Cameron Highlanders in his youth. This time, he had signed up as a sergeant in the Scouts. He and I went to look for an old friend of his, Archie Macdonald from the Lord Strathcona's Horse, the Canadian regiment of rough riders. He had been in the Camerons with Cammy and had emigrated to Canada a decade before. We found him just before they set off to the train station, but they were off that night so there was no time for a blether.

I had written half a dozen letters to Morag as we didn't know if we would be able to send or receive post from the Orange Free State, but it was early April before I finally received one from her. Short and to the point it was. She wrote that the weather had been bitter since I'd left but snowdrops were poking up and she was looking forward to the lambing, any day now. Johnny the Bochan had fixed Mairi's leaking roof and done a couple of other repairs. He liked the *craic*, and even when there was no whisky on offer he'd stayed talking until she'd had to ease him out with some oatcakes and bramble jam. She was cross with him though, because one of his many collies had had its wicked way with her devoted Sheila, who would now be having puppies in May.

The Bochan was as randy as his dog and had always had an eye for Morag. He lived by himself over in the west at Sloch, but I knew he'd be over seeking a square meal and more if he was given any encouragement. I was quite sure that Morag had mentioned him in her letter just to keep me on my toes.

My letters, in contrast, had been pages long, full of as much detail as I could cram in. We had been told our letters would be censored, but I knew Morag and the children would love to hear about the long voyage and later the wildlife – the springboks and gazelles – not to mention the flowering trees, cherry and cacti. I described seeing elephants being used to lift railway sleepers in the port and a chained lion in the street promoting Yellow Lion Brandy. There was so much to convey: the smells, the sights, the weather. Everything was so different from home and I found it impossible to do it justice.

I knew my letters would be passed around the clachan, read and re-read and so had no place for intimacy. Hers I scanned hopefully for any sign that she was missing me, but there was none. I kissed it nevertheless as I tucked it into my top pocket.

Chapter 6

Donald John, Ardnish, 1944

The door creaks open and in comes Louise, looking crestfallen. 'Canon MacNeil is away,' she says, 'Archbishop MacDonald is at Roybridge, and all the priests from the parish are with him. I was getting on the train at Borrodale and bumped into Aggy, the priest's housekeeper. She was getting the train to Arisaig but she promised to give John the train driver a message and she said he would make sure it was delivered to Canon MacNeil first thing tomorrow.' She sits by my bedside, sensing my disappointment. 'I am really sorry, Donald John. You might have to make do with your son after all.'

I clasp her hand. 'Not at all,' I say, smiling. 'You did your best.'

Angus and Louise smile between themselves; they cannot understand how much this matters to me. Angus hands her a cup of tea. 'There must be a big army exercise across at Roshven House,' Louise says, pointing to the window. 'There are searchlights sweeping across the sky and I heard the sound of aircraft passing overhead. Guns booming, machine guns rattling – did you not hear?'

Angus goes to the window to peer outside. 'I thought it was the storm,' he says. 'Oh yes, there – I see lights everywhere. There must be half a dozen ships in the bay.'

'Six ships, you say?' I am astonished.

'Looks like a full-scale war going on over there. You don't think the Germans are attacking the place?' Louise ventures nervously.

'Of course not,' Angus replies soothingly. 'It will be more training. It will likely be the SOE lot doing a final exercise before a mission.'

I'm sorry not to be able to go outside and see for myself. Over the last four years Roshven House has had thousands of men training there, and I've spent many happy hours on my doorstep sitting in the sun with my telescope trained on the canoes, or the mini submarines. Once there was even a huge battleship in the bay.

I rest my eyes for a while as Louise prepares the evening meal and am woken by Mairi's arrival. Father Angus says Mass beforehand as he always does when he is home. They all sit around my bed to eat, though it is just soup for me.

'How is Donald Angus's love life, Louise? Is he still pining for Françoise?' This is typical of my son; he likes nothing more than romance and matchmaking.

'Well,' Louise replies, 'when we last saw him, he'd been to the Canadian Embassy, the Red Cross, War Office, everywhere, trying to track her down. There's no record of her being in a prisoner of war camp so he's trying to stay optimistic. He says that if she's managed to maintain her cover as being French then no one will have a record of her. But he does think her parents will have had the "missing in action, believed dead" letter from the Canadian military about a year ago now.'

'How distressing for them all,' Angus says gently. 'But what is he doing in the Rockies?'

Louise lays down her plate. 'All he was able to tell us before he left is that the Lovat Scouts are to do a four-month winter warfare training course in Jasper. The rumour is they may be training to relieve Norway. He was delighted to be going, looking forward to being back with his old friends in the Scouts again after all his time with the SOE.'

The meal is over and the conversation moves to the subject of replacing the thatch.

'My roof is leaking again,' Mairi admits. 'I've got buckets and bowls out everywhere.'

'Maybe I could ask the army at Inverailort for some corrugated iron and we could use that instead?' Angus suggests.

'Oh, please, no,' Louise cries. 'Not that stuff. You know the folk up at Morar who swapped their thatch for wriggly tin? They regret it. They told me all the heat goes out through the roof in the winter, the place bakes in the summer, and when it rains or hails there's such a racket your head hurts and you don't get a wink of sleep. Even the tin that gets painted with bitumen rusts within a few years. Besides, where would we get new timbers from? The saw at Inverailort Castle must be rusted up from lack of use now, not to mention the fact that there's no one to do the job anyway.'

I pull the blankets up to my neck. I am cold, always cold now.

'All you all right, Father?' Louise asks. 'Can I get you anything?'

I shake my head. I won't sleep much, but I don't mind. I have my memories.

'Can I give you something to help you sleep?' Mairi asks.

'Thank you, but no need,' I reply. I'm feeling my eyelids grow heavy in any case. Mairi is very good with her potions and herbal remedies. She goes up to the lochs in the summer and gathers bogbean after it has flowered, which she then boils in water and bottles. It tastes foul but she insists that a good dose of it keeps you healthy. If you have a burn or sore, she gathers up a lichen called old man's beard, adds butter and applies it to the wound as a lotion. She has a cure for everything. These days she is feeding me a bitter nettle tea to clear my chest. I pour it away when she isn't looking. I call her the White Witch of Eriskay to her face.

Louise on the other hand is a trained nurse. Colonel Willie once told me she was known as 'the heroine of Sulva' by the Scouts in Gallipoli during the Great War. She has even won the rare Royal Red Cross Medal. She won't be having any of Mairi's magic potion nonsense. They often bicker away happily between themselves.

But it was Mairi who organised everyone on the peninsula to gather sphagnum moss to help the wounded during the Boer War. She was one of the first to realise its potential, saying they'd been using it on the islands for ever. As cotton was in short supply, the moss proved a great replacement as a blood absorbent. I remember Sheena telling me that the school would have half a day off each Wednesday and the children, plus everyone else around, would go to the bogs and collect the moss. It was laid out to dry, the insects and grass picked out, then it was put into the clean hessian bags we used for the fleeces. It was then sent by puffer to a hospital in Glasgow. By the time of the Great War the Red Cross was organising sphagnum collections all over Scotland, on a huge scale. Even Louise conceded that what she described as 'all this herbal nonsense' had been invaluable in Gallipoli.

Mairi, being an Eriskay native, had ponies in her blood, and as long as she has been at Peanmeanach the people here have been good with them. In the early years she always had a young animal that she would train to behave beautifully and carry all sorts of things: people, deer, panniers and so on. She'd sell the ponies and make good money. Once we had an unruly pony we'd got from some tinkers that kicked out at everyone, but Mairi had it sorted within days. She taught all our children and grandchildren to ride, and the confidence and ability she instilled in them has served them well.

I open my eyes and see that Angus has my old Mauser rifle in his hands, turning it over and over. He turns to me. 'Is there ammunition for this, Father?'

I shake my head. 'No longer, I'm afraid.'

Angus seems excited. 'I reckon I can get some. You never know when a deer might come down to the village. Some venison would come in handy, no doubt.'

'It won't be me using it, I'm afraid, unless it's as a crutch,' I add wryly.

Colonel Willie brought the gun over after the Boer War when he came to visit me. He thought it might come in useful, and indeed it had been. There had been a steady supply of venison over the years, first with Donald Peter and later his son dragging in a beast at dawn before the stalker, Ewen Fiadhaich, came around.

I smile at the memory and drift off to sleep.

Chapter 7

Donald John, South Africa, 1900

Training for battle filled the days at the Cape. The Lovat Scouts, just two hundred and thirty-six of us in two companies, were commanded by Major Murray. Our training involved sniping with bolt-action Lee-Metford .303 rifles. We had a telescope per man (known as a 'glass' by the stalkers), a slouch hat with one side stitched up and a square of Fraser tartan sewn on it. At Table Mountain, which overlooked the town, some of the more experienced stalkers taught the men how best to move unseen across the hillside, so they could creep up on the enemy position. Lady Lovat had given every man a pocket compass on our last day in Beauly and we practised map reading. Our days ended with a ten-mile run back to camp.

The view down onto the bay and the military camps was astounding: we could see dozens of ships, miles and miles of canvas tents divided by regiment into distinct encampments or for medical purposes. Those for the Boer prisoners were surrounded by wire and wriggly-tin guard huts. There was a constant wailing from departing trains engulfed in black smoke as they hauled carriages full of fresh recruits to Natal, the Transvaal and the Orange Free State, where the war was being fought.

Our slow and steady Highland ponies were regrettably taken away from us and quarantined due to the eye infection, and we were instead given Argentinian horses that were fast and a challenge to handle. The men were unhappy about this; many of the Highland ponies had been bred by them and were like beloved family pets. It was chaos for the first few days as the Scouts struggled to master their unbroken Argentinian mounts.

'I think this is my one, och, no, she's not – mine had a white foot,' a trooper was heard to say. The men would be dancing in circles with one foot in the stirrup as the horses spun around. The sight of my boss and others charging across the field at great speed, unable to control their horses as the Corporal of Horse bellowed instructions at them was priceless.

Within a week we were much more adept. I could gallop without being flung around like a sack of potatoes and managed some jumps while holding the reins in one hand and my rifle in the other. At the outset I'd been clinging onto my unfortunate horse's mane for dear life. Many of the islanders had been brought up doing horse races and they thoroughly enjoyed showing up the rest of us.

We watched in amazement as the regular cavalry battalions marched or charged in formation, swinging left then right, the officer wielding a sword from his horse, and some even using lances. The Guardsmen had reluctantly been talked out of their red uniforms into khaki like the rest of us and always marched briskly around the camp in step.

There were almost no women in the whole place apart

from a few nurses and those officers' wives who had
followed their husbands out but weren't allowed north.
During the day a mass of black workers moved stores and
laboured on the roads and railway, but in the evenings they
were forbidden from entering the centre of the city and
banished to the outskirts.

What we didn't know then was quite how different the
South African war would be from any that had gone before.

Chapter 8

Captain Willie MacDonald, South Africa, 1900

The war came at the right time for me. My brother Jack and I couldn't work together at the distillery any more, and he was the eldest. We had begun to argue, so the letter from Lovat asking me to join him was, I suppose, opportune.

I was glad to be back serving with my brother officers, almost all of whom had transferred from the Camerons and were great friends. Our seven weeks' training at Beaufort Castle had been hard work but tremendously exciting, and the officers' mess in the castle was like being back at boarding school. All the big houses in the area hosted parties and Dochfour even had a shoot that several of us attended. The jovial lead-up made our forthcoming trip to South Africa seem like a jolly holiday for a few months.

When we sailed in, the excitement of Cape Town itself and the impending action in the north was intoxicating. We Scouts really believed that we were the crack troops of the Imperial Army, with a role that no other regiment could do – perfectly suited for the 'shoot, run and hide' war that the Boer were carrying out.

We were told that the Boer were great horsemen and widely believed to be excellent shots. One particular skill they possessed was to shoot accurately from horseback. I was determined to master this, so I would saddle up a good horse and canter back and forth, firing at rocks for what seemed like hours. However, no amount of practice helped. I always needed at least one hand on the reins otherwise the horse sensed I was out of control and played up.

The president of the South African Republic, Paul Kruger, had anticipated the war and used the huge funds from the goldmines to buy arms from France, Germany and even Britain. They had Maxim machine guns, as did we – fantastic artillery – including four huge French guns called Long Toms that could fire accurately at a distance of five miles and land shells with great accuracy on our encampments or on besieged towns, as they had done at Ladysmith and Kimberley. The Boer snipers used German Mausers that were considerably better than our Lee-Metfords and allowed them to sit out of range and pick us off. We had been promised new Lee-Enfields which would even things up. Meanwhile, we concentrated on our horsemanship and trained for our new role as cavalry rather than infantry.

We were keen to get up to the war in the north. The Highland Brigade was commanded by General Hector MacDonald, known as 'Fighting Mac', and they'd been having an active time prior to our arrival. They lost a lot of men at Magersfontein and Paardeberg. We knew a lot of the officers there, in the Black Watch, the Gordon Highlanders, the Argyll and Sutherland, the Seaforth Highlanders and others. They didn't have a cavalry unit and they needed one urgently.

The army commander was Lord Roberts who, after a difficult start, was beginning to make headway in the campaign. Hundreds of thousands of troops were now pouring into the Cape from across the Empire. The sieges of Ladysmith and Kimberley had been relieved and our men were also moving north to capture Pretoria, where Kruger was headquartered. By the time I left for South Africa we were gaining momentum and it was widely believed that the war was being won.

However, the consensus amongst the officers in the mess was that the army had too many generals who were constantly in-fighting. They appeared incapable of agreeing on a plan, with the result that mistakes were being made – mistakes that were costing many lives. The British newspapers were attacking the prime minister and the generals with critical headlines such as '400,000 of the finest troops from across the Empire unable to beat 60,000 Boer farmers'.

Paradoxically, there was a real concern amongst us, the rank and file, that the Boer were about to capitulate. Having come all this way and having had such a fuss made over us as we left, we were desperate to have a taste of battle before the war was over, which it seemed likely would be by July, only four months away. A lot had been promised about our skill at reconnaissance and we were eager to show it was justified.

We were fortunate in that we had an excellent bunch of officers. Our Commanding Officer, Andrew Murray, was the younger brother of the Earl of Mansfield and a regular soldier in the Camerons, as I had been. He knew exactly what he was doing and the role he wanted the Scouts to

play. The officers were lairds from across the Highlands
and the men either stalkers on their estates or otherwise
well known to them (some even as poachers). There was a
strong camaraderie and respect among all the ranks. In
fact, my old friend Kenny Macdonald from Skeabost on
Skye was one of my officers. I was adjutant but was later
appointed as the commander of One Company for a while
as Simon Lovat became sick and was invalided off.

I tried to visit Simon in hospital but wasn't allowed in.
The place was full, although not a single man was there
from an injury sustained in battle. Enteric fever was raging
at the time, and I learned that far more men were dying
from disease than from gunshot. We lost one man to it
early: Sergeant Morrison, a fine soldier and a real loss to
the regiment.

Cape Town was bustling. Every hotel and guesthouse
was crammed with journalists, politicians and civil servants
out from Britain. Salesmen, too, desperate to secure
contracts for the supply of food, ammunition, train tracks,
tents and all sorts of essential goods were everywhere.
They would queue outside the Military Supplies Office
every morning to tout for trade. It was understandable, of
course; the sums of money involved were vast and the
army, at that time, profligate. This war would make the
lucky few amongst the richest men in Britain.

A number of hospital ships were tied up off Cape Town,
one of which was *Rhouma*, George Bullough's yacht from
the Isle of Rum. I'd met Bullough eighteen months before
when Kenny Macdonald and I were deer stalking with the
Frasers at Morar Lodge. It was hard to imagine him being
in South Africa now. Rumours of his decadent lifestyle had

been rife for years on the West Coast. His yacht was built to be exactly the same length as Kinloch Castle, the huge new home which he was just completing on Rum. I had heard from one of the builders how his ballroom was built with windows placed deliberately high up so that no one could see in and how it had a revolving service cupboard whereby guests would receive their drinks without any of the staff being able to witness what was going on in the room.

I was keen to reacquaint myself with the man. He was about the same age as me and I was curious. I sent a message to him asking if Kenny and I could come over for a visit. We got in a tender and set off to find *Rhouma*, eventually locating it over towards Green Point. Keen to impress, Bullough showed us around. He had had it refitted as a hospital ship, equipped for six invalid officers, twenty soldiers plus a doctor and nurses, all paid for out of his own pocket. Bullough was one of the wealthiest men in Britain and the vessel had been furnished luxuriously throughout with crystal chandeliers, beautiful paintings and mahogany furniture.

I recall Kenny teasing him. 'George, how do you expect the patients to get better now you've dismissed the brass band you normally have aboard?' We had sherry and cake with him before we left. He was about to take a ship back to England, leaving *Rhouma* in the Cape. He was delighted when we told him that if we were hit by a bullet, this was where we wanted to be – survival rates in the field hospitals being so notoriously low.

George Bullough hadn't been aware that so many of the troops in South Africa were volunteers, newly recruited for the war. He'd assumed they were all regular soldiers. 'Ah, but we're the crack forces,' I pointed out to him. 'Did you know that for every six men who applied to join the Lovat Scouts in January, only one was accepted?'

We were told that the Boer snipers specifically targeted officers. At Hart Hill, almost all the officers of the Royal Inniskilling Dragoon Guards had been shot at, long range, before the attack had properly got going, so we removed the epaulettes that signified our rank from our shoulders and painted our buttons black. We also began to carry rifles like the men, with our pistols hidden away inside our jackets or in the baggage carts.

I was fortunate that Donald John Gillies was one of my men. He was a man of the best sort, like an older brother to me in many ways. When we set off together for Beauly from Fort William in January, my mother came to wave us off. When she saw Donald John, she shook his hand and asked him to look after me. I never forgot his reply to her: 'I will put his life before mine.'

Our families have known each other for a century or more. His great-grandfather was the famous bard Ronald MacDonald of Ardnish, and he and an ancestor of mine worked for the cattle drover Corriechoillie. Both families are closely involved with the Catholic Church. My brother is a monk at Fort Augustus Abbey and has long been a great friend of Donald John and his family.

The Gillies men from Ardnish were renowned bag-pipers, descended from the hereditary pipers of Clan Macdonald of Clanranald at Castle Tioram. Ten years before the war, Donald John, at my father's funeral, led the pipers down Fort William's High Street ahead of the hearse and procession, and then at the graveside at Cille Choirill in Glen Spean as my father was laid to rest. He told me that his sons, Angus and young Donald Peter, were excellent pipers, too, already competing. I was not in the least surprised.

If anyone were to ask me what the epitome of a Highland gentleman is, I wouldn't mention the lairds or the aristocracy. I would answer: Donald John. Understated, polite, intelligent, kind and brave. He would give his last drop of water to an injured enemy soldier and his last penny to a beggar. I couldn't have had a better man at my side in war.

The family's whisky business was in a state of flux and there was no one in the regiment with whom I could discuss my concerns other than Donald John. His opinion was always carefully considered and, invariably, correct. I remember meeting him at the auction mart in Fort William four years ago when I told him we were intending to build a second distillery. True to form, after a few well directed questions he wondered if we might hold off for a few years until the existing business was stronger. However, when businesses are thriving and the outlook seems excellent, it's easy to brush aside talk of over-capacity and ignore the dark clouds on the horizon. We raised the money we needed to fund our massive expansion.

My good cheer during our first week in South Africa was brought to an abrupt end with the arrival of a letter from my older brother Jack. He was living at the lovely old Macdonald chieftain's house at Keppoch in Roybridge. He had wanted to buy the property from Mackintosh of

Mackintosh, but he wouldn't sell, which turned out to be fortunate given the news brought by his letter. He began cheerfully enough, very keen to hear my news, and wrote that if it wasn't for the need for him to try to keep the business afloat, he would have been across like a shot. It sounded to me like he wanted to escape.

He told me that the work on the extension to my new house, Blarour, was almost finished and that the bills were mounting for my return. I was desperate for news of the farm, how the livestock were faring and whether the bull I'd bought was proving a success, but knowing that my brother wouldn't be interested and had his hands full with the business, I decided to write instead to my mother and ask her to speak to the farm manager.

Jack finally got to the crux of his letter. The distillery business was not going well. There had been a collapse in the malt whisky market due to massive over-production across the industry and the crash of Pattisons in 1898. He feared it might become necessary to close the Nevis distillery. I read this with horror. It looked as though we had succumbed to the lure of the whisky bubble. We'd built the new distillery only recently and at massive expense. Despite its having the biggest production capacity in Scotland, now, it seemed, it was in serious jeopardy.

Jack enclosed several cuttings from the *Scotsman*, the *Glasgow Herald* and *The Times*. I read that the rogue Pattison brothers, Robert and Walter, who had in recent years got involved in all aspects of the whisky trade, were likely to be convicted of fraud and embezzlement and imprisoned. They had mixed bad whisky with good, inflated the quantity and value of their stock, borrowed far and wide, and then when the business failed, taken many companies down with them. One columnist wrote that he believed no new distillery would now be built in Scotland for fifty years.

The papers were full of tales of the brothers' extravagances: private trains, lavishly appointed houses in the Scottish Borders and even having five hundred African Grey parrots trained to say 'Buy Pattisons whisky', which they then gifted to publicans.

Our entire family business, Long John, was teetering. Pattisons had bought over a thousand hogsheads of our whisky and not paid for them. We had far too much unsold whisky stock, much of which was in the Pattisons warehouses, and whisky prices were plummeting. We also had substantial borrowings and were heading for massive losses, from which the business would take years to recover – if it ever did.

'What else could possibly go wrong?' Jack wrote. 'I need you back here. I can manage the distilleries in the Fort and you could go to Edinburgh and London, track down our casks and get them into warehouses we control, then calm down the banks we owe money to. With a full day of travel to get anywhere I am struggling and can't be in two places at once. The Scouts are a volunteer force – surely you can resign and head back?'

I laid down the letter, feeling sick in the stomach. We'd followed the herd and were suffering the consequences. What would our canny father be thinking from up above?

Jack reported that our mother was well though she never ceased worrying about her son at the Front, like mothers all across Britain. She considerately arranged for both the *Oban Times* and the London *Times* to be mailed to me during the campaign, and both were fought over in the officers' mess. I wondered how much Jack told her about the worrying state of the business. She was bound to have read about Pattisons as it had been listed on the Stock Exchange and its collapse had been a front-page story, but I was sure Jack would have done what he could to shield her from the worst.

The odd thing about being away at war was how much one craved news from home. Even though one may have just seen an hour-old impala being nursed by its mother, or a rainbow of remarkable clarity, neither miracle would stop the troopers' stampede towards the wagon bearing the weekly post. I felt guilty being out here in this sunlit wide-open land, having the time of my life and leaving poor Jack alone to fight to save the business.

Donald John came in with a message that the officers were to meet at the mess tent at 5 p.m. for orders.

'Do you have a minute, Gillies?' I asked, pointing to the canvas stool opposite me. He sat down and I explained my dilemma. 'The whisky industry is in turmoil. We have a large number of whisky casks stored in warehouses owned by crooks, whisky prices are collapsing and the British Linen Bank is putting pressure on us to repay their loans. Jack wants me to go back home. Yet on the other hand, Lovat is in hospital, we're short of experienced officers, I'm both adjutant and squadron commander, and we're about to go into battle. If I leave, Major Murray will have a real problem and I fear that men could die if an officer with no experience in action were to lead them.'

We discussed the pros and cons of the situation but came to no firm conclusion. Donald John urged me to write a letter of support to Jack to reassure him that I had complete trust in him.

I proceeded to the mess tent feeling better for having shared my problems. There, I was instructed to lead half our battalion to Bloemfontein with instructions to go to the help of General MacDonald. I had no choice. I had to stay here, at least for a few months. Our campaign was expected to be short and lives were at risk. The commanding officer depended on me. My mind was made up.

I sat down to write a short note to Jack immediately so as to catch the mail before we left Cape Town.

My dear Jack,

You paint a bleak picture with your news of the collapse at Pattisons and the resulting problems faced by us and the other distilleries. There can be few more capable people than you, and I can think of no one I would have more confidence in to manage the business in difficult times.

It is with regret, however, that I must inform you that I cannot come back, I'm afraid, much though I would like to. We are short of experienced officers due to sickness, and the Scouts are now being sent to the aid of the Highland Brigade, who are in a tight spot. I went to see our friend Simon Lovat, who is in hospital, but was stopped from going in to the ward due to the risk of infection. He is in a bad way, and I beseech you to pray for his recovery.

Give my love to Mother.

Your loving brother,

Willie

Chapter 9

Donald John, South Africa, May 1900

We had been in Cape Town for a month. Winter was approaching, and finally we were off to war. Our squadron boarded a train and we headed six hundred and fifty miles north to Bloemfontein. This journey, which apparently took less than a day and night for civilian trains before the war, somehow took us three days. We were shunted into sidings from time to time, and we would take the opportunity to feed and exercise the horses that were tethered in the accompanying freight wagons and get a brew going. In the evenings, the squadron cook made us a proper meal while the train was refuelled with coal in a freight yard. The Africans who had been captured alongside the Boer were being set up in camps alongside the railways and they were employed to lug the coal, repair the train tracks and so on. With trains going through at a rate of four every hour each way, these railway networks were the arteries of South Africa and essential to the war effort. The Boer Commando frequently blew up the track and so all the bridges had army pickets guarding them. The trains had Maxim machine guns mounted front and back, and we had our rifles to hand.

The trains were impressive. They were manufactured in Glasgow and York, and were twice as long as any of the ones we had at home. The coal for the engines was mined in a town called Glencoe, in Natal, which was near another town called Dundee. I discovered connections to Scotland everywhere. I even saw two of A. & J. Main's tin tabernacles. In many ways we felt quite at home, especially during the cold nights as we shivered under our single-issue blankets.

I recall one occasion, just a few hours before we were due to disembark, when our train pulled over to allow another, heading south, to pass. We were stationary for a long time. A hospital train pulled up alongside, its open windows inches from ours. Gaunt, grey, sweat-covered faces stared back at us, most with filthy, blood-soaked bandages wrapped around their heads. In the background we could hear the cries of many in desperate pain. Our men reached through the windows and proffered sweets, cigarettes and tobacco, with barely a word said. We moved off, shaken. The reality of war was sinking in.

The train stopped again at what was no more than an empty platform in the veld, about an hour south of Bloemfontein. Captain MacDonald ordered us all out. Our kit and horses were unloaded, lines for the horses quickly strung out, and then Cammy had the hundred of us form into close ranks. There was much chatter amongst the men about what was going on; even the officers didn't seem to know.

It soon became clear. I had heard tales of an extraordinary man – an American named Burnham – while we were in the Cape. He had proposed to Major Murray that the

Scouts would benefit from training and offered his services. We were to wait here for him.

After an hour on parade in the blistering sun, into sight came a single horseman at a slow gallop. He sat on the mount as if he was glued to it. On his head was a Stetson, round his waist an ammunition belt with ivory-handled six-shooter pistols strapped to each hip, and he wore a black coat with no insignia whatsoever. He was small and slight, with piercing eyes and a bushy moustache.

The men looked on in incredulity as he halted and began to address us in his drawling Minnesotan accent. 'Good day,' he began. 'My name is Frederick Russell Burnham, Fred to you. I am the Chief of Scouts. I report directly to Lord Roberts, Commander of the Army in South Africa. I've never been a soldier, British or American. I have been a cowboy, a horse rustler, a gold prospector and a hunter, and I've tracked and been tracked by the best scouts in the world: the American Indians.'

Our mouths dropped open in amazement.

'Y'all will be under my command for three days. We're going to set up camp down by a *spruit* nearby, and I'm going to tell you how the Boer fight, teach you some scouting tricks, and then you're going to get back on the train and head into Bloemfontein. But the main thing I'm going to teach y'all is how important it is to know your enemy, and with that knowledge, how you will beat him.'

Burnham's information and expertise grew more and more valuable to us as the war went on. He had a British sergeant and three corporals working for him, and over the days that followed they taught us how to track the enemy and cover our own tracks. We learned how to braid ropes, throw a lasso over a man from horseback, navigate at night without a compass and map using the stars, how to use explosives, how to withstand torture, and how to snap-shoot without aiming. Captain MacDonald finally mastered shooting a pistol accurately from either hand at full gallop, which pleased him no end.

Burnham didn't socialise with anyone. When all the work was done, late into the night, he would disappear into the bush. But one night his sergeant told us Burnham's story. He had grown up the son of a missionary on a Sioux reservation in Minnesota. He had been a tracker for the US Army during the Apache wars, had met Baden-Powell during the Matabeleland wars a decade before, and Lord Roberts had asked him to return from Alaska, where he was prospecting for gold, to become Chief of Scouts. He didn't smoke or drink as he believed it would not only make him smell but also dull his senses, and he drank very little water so he could learn to cope without it when he needed to.

Later, as we headed up to Bloemfontein to join the Highland Brigade, we Scouts couldn't stop talking about him. We had all been sceptical at first, but this had quickly changed to admiration, to the point where there wasn't a man amongst us who wasn't hugely impressed with his knowledge and his teaching. He had the makings of a legend among us.

When Lovat returned from sick leave, Captain MacDonald sat him down after patrol one evening and talked about the eccentric and inspirational American. Lovat drank in everything he was told about the man. If it wasn't for the fact that Burnham was almost fatally wounded behind enemy lines in Pretoria and then sent to England to recuperate, I am sure that Lovat's charm would have lured Burnham back to teach us more.

Captain MacDonald was later heard to say to Lord Lovat that Number One Company had learned more of the art of scouting in three days from Fred Burnham than they had learned in Beauly in a month – and that those three days would have saved many of our lives. In turn Burnham described our men as 'half wolf and half jackrabbit'. We weren't sure if that was a compliment but we decided to take it as one.

Chapter 10

Captain Willie MacDonald, South Africa, 1900

After the excitement of Burnham's training we had a short train trip north, where we made camp in Bloemfontein amidst thousands of men, horses and wagons. There were those newly arrived from the Cape, like us, preparing to be sent off to join depleted brigades, as well as battalions of seasoned veterans who were having a week's leave to recover. And, of course, there were thousands of support personnel who followed the men into battle. It was an enormous, teeming tented city.

There were turban-wearing Sikhs, New Zealanders, Australians, Canadians, even Negroes from the far-off Caribbean. Many of the soldiers were on their way to capture Pretoria and Johannesburg where there was already a brigade of American Irish plus German, Belgian, Dutch and Russian regiments. What everyone had initially believed to be no more than a small number of Boer farmers trying to break free from British rule was now turning into a massive struggle between the British Empire and the Boer.

While the majority of British soldiers were of the highest calibre, quite a few of those joining the volunteer regiments had only done so because of the high pay on offer, and there appeared to have been no effort to sort the wheat from the chaff. Some members of the Imperial Yeomanry, who had been recently recruited in England and forwarded to the front, were unable either to ride or shoot when they arrived at the Cape. Our sergeant heard that later, when a shipload of these returned warriors reached England, they were described as 'street loafers and disease-ridden rapscallions'.

Our orders were to join the Highland Brigade under Fighting Mac; they were on their way north towards Johannesburg. We took a train onwards to Kroonstad, which was to be followed by a thirty-mile ride up to Heilbron. We still hadn't met up with the rest of the Scouts; Major Murray and Two Company had been delayed waiting for fresh horses in the Cape. The plan was to catch up with General Paget and his brigade, who were a day ahead of us, and go with them to relieve the possibly encircled Highland Brigade at Heilbron.

Kroonstad, like every railway town, was buzzing. There were troops camped everywhere and injured men were being carted towards any hotel, school or church that had space for them. The streets were so congested with oxen, mules, horses and people that you had to push your way through. The few shops that were open had sold out of anything that could conceivably be eaten or drunk, and we noted the extortionate prices that were being asked for the most basic provisions.

We spent four days in Kroonstad. One night we heard shouting and the noise of hooves, so we leapt from our cots and rushed outside. Two hundred horses – perhaps spooked by something – had broken out of their *kraal* and were now thundering through the camp at full gallop. I discovered the exact position of every picket peg with my bare feet in the dark that night.

On another day, a horse race was organised. Anyone who could find a guinea could enter, and at least a hundred did. The course began at the church, then ran out of town on the Winburg Road for about three miles, around a hillock (a *kopje*) and back again. The street was lined with thousands of every nationality; the regiments all cheering their own. The winner, a corporal in Brabant's Horse, was awarded all the entry money, enough to buy a house when he got home.

We camped beside the Valsch River, where there was a grand pool. The men swam and bathed daily for the week we were there. At one point, Donald John and I accompanied two of our men, who had succumbed to dysentery, to the hospital, and when we arrived there we noticed that it was called the Scottish National Red Cross Hospital. All under canvas, it was spacious, generously furnished and efficiently run. Our two men confessed that once they were admitted they would be unlikely to want to join us again.

Disease was rife, although the Lovat Scouts were comparatively lucky. When Simon Lovat rejoined us after recovering from his bout of illness, the men were gathered together and given a strict talking to. On no account was dirty water to be drunk – *ever* – even if we'd been a day without, for as sure as hell it would lead to misery and quite likely death. We observed other regiments' men who didn't give a damn how dirty the water was, as long as it was wet.

When we finally set off on the big trek to Heilbron, we were anxious to bring along as many supplies as we could for the Highland Brigade, who would by now be running low. I organised two extra bowsers of water, five wagons of food and ammunition and twenty oxen to pull them.

On our very first day, just out of Kroonstad, Donald John, Sergeant Cameron and I were at the rear of our small column when we found ourselves further out than we should have been. I halted to investigate a five-inch gun that had been abandoned and was trying to disable it permanently when I heard Donald John calling out. Out of the corner of my eye I saw a movement only a hundred yards away – a stirring in a bush, perhaps a rifle being moved into position to take a shot at us.

I vaulted onto my horse and the three of us wheeled away, bullets flying all around us. It was about half a mile until we could catch up with our rear guard but we had a dozen Boer on our tail and gaining on us as we galloped towards safety. It was immediately clear how much faster and in better condition the Boer horses were than ours. Donald John and I were ahead and nearly safe when I looked behind to see Sergeant Cameron surrounded by Boer – a lucky shot had knocked his horse down. The Afrikaners were swarming around him like hornets. We wheeled around and galloped towards them, but bullets were singing past our heads and we knew it would be madness to keep going.

We saw them haul Cameron onto the back of a horse and ride off. He didn't appear to be badly injured, but I was shaken by the incident. My conscience pricked for not going to his rescue, but the men assured us we had done the right thing. It was said that the Boer behaved like gentlemen towards their prisoners so he would likely be unharmed.

There were constant skirmishes on our journey. Those same Boer would come up to the rear of our wagon trail and try to capture them. At one point a wheel came off one of our wagons and several hours were spent shifting its contents onto another already fully loaded cart while the Boer circled us, trying to find a weak spot. Reluctantly, we had to abandon a ton of supplies, doubtless ferried off by the enemy come nightfall.

The countryside was predominantly flat, rolling ground. An advance party of four would ride ahead to a rise, take their glasses out and scan the area. Then, as we moved forward, the wagons followed. General MacDonald was already at Heilbron, but it wasn't clear whose hands the town was in. What we did know for certain was that seven thousand Boer were in the area and nothing had been heard from the Highland Brigade for almost a month.

Donald John and I dashed back and forth between the wagons, fighting the rearguard action with flankers who were under the command of Lieutenant Ellice. At one point, Lieutenant Ewan Grant was at full canter when his horse stumbled into an aardvark hole in the long grass. The animal pitched forward, broke its leg and threw Grant heavily to the ground, dislocating his shoulder. Within five minutes the horse had been shot and a new one found, Grant's shoulder was pulled back into position, and we were mounted and off again.

On the second day of the trek we were in the saddle for almost fourteen hours, with only an hour's break. Our men were exhausted, having ridden under a hot sun on only one ration biscuit and some bully beef. We finally set up camp in a hollow by a river as the evening temperature fell. Pickets were sent out to the ridge around us to watch the Boer moving around their campfires, only a mile or two away. But no fire for us. The men stretched out, too tired to talk.

As night fell, the men operated in pairs, one struggling to sleep because of the cold and anxiety, and the other on watch. Every man had to sleep beside his saddled horse and we were ordered to keep our boots on and our rifles by our sides. Burnham's advice was fresh in our minds and we were extra vigilant; it seemed a certainty that the Boer would take advantage of our vulnerability and attack at night.

We were lucky to be undisturbed that night. However, the next morning we had the Boer at our backs from the start. Half our men positioned themselves behind the convoy, desperately staving them off as the rest of us sped towards the town as fast as we could, considering the crawling pace at which oxen travel. Our men, ten to a troop, would lie on a *kopje* and shoot at the Boer as they came over the rise a good three hundred yards away. This would cause them to dismount and fire back. Hitting their horses was almost as important to us. Then our men would move back to our force with another troop of Scouts already in position at the top of the next rise.

I overheard Johnny Mackenzie, a stalker from Strathglass, use the language of the deer forest as he spied through his glass while another sniped at a Boer: 'The first was a wee bit low and to the right. The second hit him high on the body.'

Our baggage, the oxen wagons, half a dozen cattle that we'd commandeered on the way and some spare horses continued to creep at two miles an hour despite the natives rushing around and cracking bull whips. We were encouraged by the knowledge that two hundred thousand rounds of .303 bullets and fresh provisions would be well received by the general when we arrived. We would have arrived in less than half the time, however, if we hadn't had to transport the lot.

The last two miles were perilous. We had to travel across open ground and through our telescopes we saw many armed men ahead. Unless these were Highlanders we were in for a lot of trouble, but the onslaught at our rear continued, so we had no choice but to keep going. Luckily, it turned out to be a picket of Seaforths, on their way out to help us.

We were the heroes of the hour and General MacDonald made a real fuss of us. He called out to me as we arrived, 'By Jove, we were thankful when we saw you fellows ride calmly into the town. What have you got in those wagons?'

The brigade was down to half-rations, with scarcely any ammunition left when we arrived. The Highland Brigade was virtually all infantry with almost no cavalry, just a small Cape troop who were overused and exhausted. And with the Boer surrounding the town and their ability to outmanoeuvre foot soldiers, Fighting Mac had been well and truly trapped.

We were given three days off-duty to recover but the brigade needed both our manpower and our horses so we were constantly in demand. We were sent to provide cover for engineers, to mend the telegraph wires, or to hunt for livestock. One of our young officers, Lieutenant Fraser-Tytler, was on patrol when he came across some African boys guarding about sixty head of cattle and five hundred sheep. In a cloud of dust, Fraser-Tytler and his men drove the animals back to camp and were only saved from the Boer by some Seaforths who went out to bring them in. One trooper, a Glencoe Macdonald, remarked that his cattle-raiding ancestors would have been proud; it had quite awakened his predatory instincts.

We were popular that night. It had been weeks since the besieged garrison had had meat, and there was plenty of it. All across the camp, men would come up to us and shake our hands, full of congratulations. The next day, General MacDonald ordered some cattle to be butchered and distributed to the couple of hundred civilians in the town.

We were sent out as scouts from time to time, but only for a few hours a day. Donald John and I tried to find the location of a big gun that was shelling the town. We finally found it inside a tumbledown house, looking like a gigantic black roof beam poking through the wall. The Cape Troop and the Eastern Province Horse went out the next morning and took it.

A picket reported that there was a white flag flying near a *kraal*, so we sent out a patrol to see what was going on. As they approached, they encountered a tremendous volley of shots from about thirty Boer – the white flag was merely being used to mark the range, it seemed. What treachery.

One of the Scouts was sent to take a message to General Methuen of the First Division, who was about thirty miles away, and he returned with some useful information about the Boer positions. I was then ordered to recce the ground for Methuen and so, without any baggage to slow us down, a troop went out, found the best route and, with our help, Methuen and his thousand men were able to fight their way through to Heilbron. The next morning the pickets reported no sign of the enemy and it became clear that the Boer had disappeared overnight and the siege had lifted.

It was while we were at Heilbron that we learned that the Boer capital, Pretoria, had fallen to the British, but Kruger had escaped. Now everyone was speculating that the war had only weeks to run before the Boer capitulated. We had time on our hands after this, and I took the opportunity to walk around the town, swim in the lake and catch up with my friends in the Argyll and Seaforth regiments.

Our camp was located beside a beautiful lake on the edge of Heilbron, in the shade of gum trees. I relaxed there with the Lochaber men as they enjoyed their tea and cigarettes. Their constant preoccupation was running out of tobacco. We sat around the fire talking about the countryside and what great farming land lay all around us. There was even talk of coming back after the war and setting up a Highland colony; the men felt that the place had the potential to become the best cattle and sheep farming land in the world.

The secret to farming success out there was ensuring a good water supply. If a farm name finished with the word '*fontein*', there would be a fountain or spring. The only real menace were the jackals, who would be after the sheep all night unless you had men out. Other men were minded to join Baden-Powell, who was building up the South African police.

Several of the island men in the Scouts only spoke Gaelic and poor communication with the officers could lead to all sorts of misunderstanding. I would often call upon Donald John to be my translator. Donald John always had a flair for languages; it ran in his family. He became determined to learn Dutch; there were always prisoners to be interrogated or transported, and he decided he could be more useful if he could converse with them. We had been at Heilbron for a couple of days when he encountered a captured Boer who had been a schoolteacher and was keen to improve his English. Donald John would go over to his compound twice a day. The Boer, named Coen, had a bayonet wound in his thigh and Donald John was able to get him iodine and fresh bandages. He told Donald John he had fought alongside the British at Rorke's Drift against the Zulus twenty years ago as a lad and had a great affection for the Tommies, as he called the British. Coen sorely wished the war would end. He believed nothing good would come of it and the British, with their vast numbers, would win sooner rather than later. He said that many of the Boer would fight to the bitter end as a matter of honour. Donald John relayed this information to me and I must confess I was not surprised.

Chapter 11

Donald John, Ardnish, 1944

The family goes about their day. Louise comes to talk for a while; I sense they must have agreed to take it in turns to look after me. I feel content; it's pleasant listening to her, feeling her young hand on mine.

Louise loves to talk. She tells me about how the farm-house at Laggan is in a better state than it has been for years, how lucky her son is to have the farm tenancy for Ardnish when the war ends, and how kind it was of Colonel Willie's son to give a guarantee to the Arisaig Estate on his behalf. And how lucky Donald Angus is that the women are looking after it for him in the meantime, although he will doubtless make more of it eventually. The farm could definitely hold more cattle and sheep on the place than it does currently.

But then she pauses. I suspect she is thinking of Donald Peter, her late husband and my beloved son. She seldom talks about him to me, perhaps knowing it still hurts after all those years.

'Do you still miss my son, Louise? You never mention him.' Old people can say what they like, speak what other people fear to, so I venture the question.

Tears well in her eyes and her hand clasps mine tighter. 'I do miss him, Father, desperately. But it's been so long now, sometimes I wonder if the boy I see in my mind was just a dream. Was he really like I remember him, I wonder?'

She rocks gently back and forth on the edge of the bed. 'He would have so loved Donald Angus and been so incredibly proud of him – his piping successes and doing so well in the army. The father and son have all the same characteristics. The way they sweep their hair back, the tilt of the head when they're listening intently, even the words they use. How can that be?'

She talks about how wonderful it is that Donald Angus loves Ardnish as much as his father did and how he yearns for it to flourish, to be full of children's voices once again. He wants to find a wife who is happy with her own company, who would enjoy the remoteness and wildness – a girl who will love him and this place and share his dreams for it.

'He told me once' – she smiles – 'when he was young that he wants to have eight children, all with red hair, and then the school board would have to open the school again. Can you imagine!

'It's such a shame that he found this Canadian girl and fell for her. His first love, yet he never tells her and then she gets captured.'

She looks at me, willing me to say that the girl, Françoise, will be all right.

But I don't want her to have false hope. 'We don't know anything for sure, Louise. All we can do is keep praying for her.' Privately, I know her experience will have been horrific. She was very likely tortured and then taken to a death camp. I've seen the newspaper articles about the German concentration camps; few came out alive from those hell-holes. I wonder if she managed to keep her secrets about the resistance fighters and their families; if not, dozens would be arrested, and there would probably be reprisals against the village. Donald Angus hadn't mentioned anything about reprisals when he was home. I had told him as gently as I could to stop pining for her and get on with his life when he was home on leave, but he didn't want to hear it: he was determined to keep searching.

We sit in companionable silence for a while, each with our own thoughts.

'I'd love to have met her,' says Louise after a while. 'I wonder what her feelings for my son were. She can't have helped falling for him, don't you think?'

I nod. 'She'll be a grand lass. He has good taste in women.'

Louise sighs and gazes out of the window. 'It's turning to snow now,' she murmurs. 'It's coming down thick and fast out there. Can you see it, Donald John? I hope Angus isn't too far off. Didn't he say he was going over to Laggan?'

We make sporadic conversation over the next hour. The wind is driving the snow against the glass, and I can hardly see out.

'It'll be dark soon. I wish he was back,' Louise says.

It is dusk when Angus eventually returns, the door shooting back in the wind and a flurry of snow coming in with him. He stamps the snow off his boots.

Louise fusses over him. They head over to Mairi's house, promising to be back with supper shortly. Louise is anxious about the animals in the deep snow and how furious Morag would be if she came back to lots of dead sheep.

In the silence, my fingers twitch a tune and I think about Donald Angus and his piping. Ever since he won at Inverness, he has become well known in the piping world, and is constantly asked to give lessons and to write tunes.

I remember going to Mass at Our Lady of the Braes, well before the war, and near the back sat a good-looking young man I'd never seen before. He introduced himself after the service. He was a Canadian, by the name of Ranald Macdonald, from Inverness County in Cape Breton. He'd come to the Braes hoping to meet my grandson and myself. His people had left Roybridge in the 1820s and were related to the famous Cranachan brothers. The five unwed brothers were known as the strongest men in Scotland and legendary in the Highlands. He'd visited their house and Cille Choirill church, which the Cape Breton people had raised money to rebuild. He was eager to discuss piping with us, so I invited him to come and stay at Peanmeanach, telling him that Donald Angus, who was in Mallaig staying with his uncle, would be back home the next day.

Ranald planned to stay the night, but he ended up staying for two weeks. He worked in a sawmill at home, and while he was with us he expertly cut and dragged firewood from all around.

Ranald knew many old Highland tunes, long forgotten in these parts, some of which we'd heard of but had never heard played.

My fingers were too stiff and my mind too old to learn new tunes, but I enjoyed listening to Ranald and Donald Angus chantering away all day. They learned a lot from each other. Ranald had heard of a woman called Sheena and many of the others who had emigrated from this area, through his fiddling friends. They were now settled on the east coast of Canada. When my wife enquired about Sheena and said she was without a family, he looked confused; we agreed it must be a different one. I recall asking if he knew of the Miramichi Macdonalds down at Mull River, friends of our Sheena and Cranachans like himself. 'They'd be related to Colonel Willie and the Archbishop as likely as not,' I told him. It turned out he had indeed heard of them, and agreed what fine people they were.

Sheena mentioned Ranald in subsequent letters over the years and I heard from her that he had died just before the war broke out. He had been cutting lumber deep in the woods, there was a sudden heavy snowfall, and he became disorientated. Sadly, he never made it back to safety. We were all terribly upset at the news as he'd been a wonderful guest and acquaintance – someone whom Donald Angus would have enjoyed meeting in Canada.

They are all huddled around the fire now. With the coal added to the peat, it's blazing. The wind is rattling the windows but it's cosy in here, although my eyes sting with the acrid smoke.

Angus brings me some photographs from the kist and I peer at them in the dim light. There is an image of several youngsters, smiling and excited, arms interlocked, twirling around outside, in a field somewhere. In the background I can see an elderly piper with short black hair. Angus turns the photograph over and I see the inscription: 'Danny and Joe MacDonald, the Mull River MacDonalds. Aonghus Dhu piping.'

'Isn't it amazing,' says Angus, 'that thousands of miles across the Atlantic hundreds of thousands of people call themselves Scots, speak Gaelic, and pipe, fiddle and dance the same way as it's done right here? There are MacDonalds, Gillies and MacLellans going to Mass and living in villages called Arisaig, Glencoe and Inverness. It really is a new Scotland. What a shame we never went over. Sheena would have shown us a great time.'

'I couldn't agree more,' I reply.

Louise rummages in the kist. 'There's a letter along with that photograph,' she says, picking it up and reading aloud. '"Went with friends to a parish picnic at Mabou where we danced. Tried the step-dance for the first time."' Louise glances over at me and smiles. 'She goes on to write that "Black Angus was the best-known piper around but he was also a great fiddler".'

Angus is interested for another reason. 'Look!' he exclaims. 'He has the bag on his right shoulder, and his right hand's on top. His fingers are all crooked, too. I'll bet he never learned to read music.'

We study other photographs, all of them small and dog-eared: a picnic by Lake Ainslie, adults, children and a large red-coated Labrador. 'That's Ruadh, Sheena told us once. What a handsome animal he is.'

And here's Sheena framed in the doorway of a pretty little cottage, holding a young girl's hand. An old woman stands beside them. Written on the back, we read 'Mrs MacEachern'.

'That's where Sheena lives. Isn't she lucky having such a bonny house?' Mairi says.

'Who's the girl?' I ask.

'No idea, maybe a friend's daughter,' Angus replies dismissively. 'Doesn't Sheena look well?'

'Your mother was never happier than when Sheena came home to visit,' I say. 'She cried all the way back in the train after waving her off in Glasgow. She was convinced it would be the last time she'd ever see her.'

'Sheena said that Danny, Joe and the piper are all Cranachan MacDonalds, from Roybridge way,' Angus says. 'She wrote to me about them. She said something along the lines of "whatever their material condition, a sense of dignity was bred in the bone". I've always remembered it.'

My eyelids are heavy.

'I'll check on himself,' I hear Mairi whisper.

'He's asleep,' she says, but I am not. I can hear her topping up the fire, and then she turns on the wireless. The clipped BBC voice announces the ten o'clock news.

It is sobering. The Russians have relieved the siege of Leningrad, and it is believed that two million civilians there have died of starvation and disease. And the British destroyer HMS *Janus* has been sunk off the Anzio beachhead in Italy.

'It's hard to credit we're winning, isn't it?' says my son.

'My Lord,' says Mairi, 'What a shocking number of deaths. It's beyond belief. Will this terrible war never end?'

The storm is still battering against the window. I don't remember snow like this for a good three years. There was a hell of a winter in '41, when we were snowbound for two weeks and the sea froze. It had been novel for the first few days, but then we started to worry about the animals starving and realised we had precious little food for ourselves. It was bitterly cold, the snow two feet deep in places, but with clear blue skies and not a breath of wind. We had to take shovels and dig out the sheep that were huddled inside one of the ruined crofts.

Captain Andrew MacDonald was back from the Faroe Islands on a visit at that time, training with the SOE at Inverailort Castle, and one afternoon we suddenly heard the deep throb of an engine and hurried out to see what was going on. Into the bay came a landing craft, with Captain MacDonald waving from the front as the bow was lowered. He and several soldiers unloaded provisions for us, as well as a few sacks of turnips for the livestock. He even had a bottle of Long John for myself. Never was there a more welcome visitor at Peanmeanach.

He was carrying skis, I remember, and was planning to ski back to Arisaig. He showed us the sealskin strips attached to the base. They stopped the skis slipping backwards and meant he could travel as quick as a man could run. The Lovat Scouts had been issued with the ski equipment, along with white fur-lined jackets and trousers, in the Faroe Islands, where they had been sent to train before their mission to relieve Norway.

The captain stayed overnight, providing an excellent excuse to have a wee dram. As we sat by the fire, we used the kindling axes to cut the turnips into smaller pieces for the sheep. He told us how the regiment was getting on in the Faroe Islands, how they were constantly getting strafed by German planes, and spending their time trying to blow up drifting mines. It was a garrison job and the men were frustrated; they wanted to get some action soon. It didn't matter whether it was in Norway or even France.

I remember the taste of that whisky well – was it the last I'd had? Maybe not, come to think of it. Donald Angus had a smidgen in a hip flask which he passed round last summer when he came over.

Captain Andrew was impressed with Donald Angus, telling us he was well regarded by everyone. He reckoned our lad would thrive in the SOE and vowed to try to get him signed up as soon as he got back. Morag was delighted with this plan. The SOE were based all around us at the big houses of Roshven, Inverailort and Arisaig, and we would get to see him.

The next morning, we watched as the captain glided off effortlessly, through the snow and away uphill through the trees.

Mairi has made some tasty broth but I struggle to get it down. After the fire is damped down, they head off to sleep, leaving me and Broch the collie to watch the embers flickering in the draught.

I sleep fitfully, coughing and spluttering through the long night, until I am woken by the sound of the door opening.

'Good morning, Donald John. How are you today?' Mairi says in her soft lilting accent as she comes in, brushing the snow off her coat. Instinctively she adds a bit more water to Louise's porridge and gives it a stir. 'It's as flat as a prairie out there, what with all the snow,' she says. 'All the hillocks and holes have been levelled.'

I'd love nothing more than to get up and have a look myself.

Angus comes in with a creel of peat in his hands. 'I don't think your priest will be coming to see us today, Father. He'd never find the path and I doubt the train will be running.' He replenishes the stack by the fire. 'This is the only creel in good shape now,' he says. 'The bottom has fallen out of the old one. We need you better, Father, so you can make some more.'

I nod weakly. I pride myself on my creel-making. It's a good couple of years since I made one; the last was for

Mairi. It's one of the things I can do well despite my injury.
Louise and I used to take the pony over to Sloch where there
is lots of straight hazel – perfect for creels. We would cut a
couple of bundles of rods, strap them behind me and ride
back. I would then get to work, peeling the bark off them
and stacking them in the shed to dry. Creels were good for
barter. There was a cobbler in Lochailort who made good
sturdy boots and I made an exchange with him: a pair of
boots for two creels and a fine *cromach* I'd made. It was the
first time he'd made a pair of left-footed boots, he told me.

The time passes quickly. It's a perfect winter's day, with
not a breath of wind and the sunshine reflecting on the
snow making the inside of the house surprisingly bright. I
am worried that my wife won't get here for days, with the
snow so deep. The lost sheep are discovered, tucked safely
in one of the tumbledown black houses, and the two
women and Angus are in and out all day long, cheerful due
to the invigorating weather.

In the hours when I am alone, I contemplate how Morag
will manage when I die and my pension stops. There hasn't
been a lot I could contribute to the family coffers over the
years since I lost my leg. I used to make about fifty peat
creels every year, but with so few people on the peninsula
now and with coal being available as part of our rations,
there just isn't the demand any more. I pride myself,
immodestly, that the *cromachs* I make are the best in the
Highlands. When old Astley-Nicholson was alive and
bringing stalking guests over to Ardnish they never left
without a stick and me without a guinea or two in my
pocket and a smile on my face.

Chapter 12

Captain Willie MacDonald, South Africa, 1900

I took a patrol of ten men to a farm near Winburg. Two white families occupied two separate dwellings: four women, four children and their servants. The women were hospitable, making us tea and offering husks, popular over here in the same way oatcakes are at home. Donald John conversed with them in his passable Dutch and we learned that their husbands were away helping on a nearby farm and would be back soon, maybe that evening. I reassured them that no harm would come to them and their property was safe.

The two houses were most attractive – white-painted wood with green corrugated roofs and verandas, or *stoeps* – and surrounded by stunning acacia trees with bright yellow flowers. Massive gum trees overhung a dam which lay just below the site. Although it was March and getting colder at night, it was still infernally hot during the day, so we all took a dip in the water that night, before supper.

On patrol, we had taken to what the natives called meal-ies. The dish consisted of corn cut from the cob, which was cooked in water and then mashed up and eaten with milk

– a sort of delicious African porridge. I bought ten eggs, milk, bread and dried beef from the farmers' wives for six shillings and we ate well that night, finishing up with melons and figs which we found around the grounds. There were orange and lemon trees in the fields, too, but their fruit wasn't yet ripe.

That night, tucked up snugly on a bed of hay in a barn, with men on sentry duty outside, I said to Kenny Macdonald that this must be one of the most tranquil and beautiful places on earth. I declared I would return with my family some day, but until then this place would be my secret. Oblivious to the war that night, I had a contented feeling as I drifted off. I remember a cat coming in beside me and curling up against my back.

Early the next morning, the Sussex Regiment arrived and the peace was brutally shattered. They'd been commanded to torch the place. I remonstrated fiercely with the colonel but to no avail. The women were given ten minutes to gather their belongings, and then we could only watch, dumbstruck, as the houses were torched and their dog shot. The looks the women gave me conveyed their sense of betrayal and disgust.

I harnessed a horse to a trap, so that the women could load it up for their trek to the camp. I felt ashamed at having broken my promise. Just then, one of the infantry-men who had been searching an outbuilding gave a shout and the commanding officer rushed to join him. They emerged shortly afterwards carrying boxes of ammunition. I turned towards the women, astonished. They could no longer look me in the eye. I must have looked a gullible fool in everyone's eyes, I must say.

My men and I rode off in silence, to return to our camp. Accompanying us throughout this period was a correspondent from the *Morning Post* called H. W. Blundell, so we knew that all our actions would be reported and that my mother and everyone who knew us would read about it.

In my mother's letters to me she would mention articles that referenced in detail our occasional predicaments – events that I had, of course, played down in my correspondence. For example, once I wrote that we had ridden to join General MacDonald at Heilbron and left it at that. But she promptly sent me a cutting from a new newspaper that had just been launched called *The Daily Express*. It described in vivid detail how the Lovat Scouts were harried and shot at all week as they fought their way through with vital supplies and how the men had their horses shot from beneath them as they raced for the town through the middle of an eight thousand-strong Boer army to a heroes' welcome from General MacDonald and the Highland Brigade. Suffice it to say, Mother demanded a bit more candour in my future letters home.

She wrote only one line about the whisky business: 'Jack says things are very difficult at the distillery right now, and has written asking for you to come home to help.' I did not rise to the bait. Jack knew my rationale for staying here.

Blundell built our trust with his dispassionate reporting. He was unusual in this respect. Many others were exaggerating acts of bravery and glorifying the war in the most jingoistic terms, while downplaying the reality of our daily conditions out here. Wild and irresponsible rumours in the press only upset those dearest to us at home.

The night after we broke through, Blundell and I had
dinner at Heilbron with Fighting Mac. The general told
me what a commendable job we had done, that we were
an integral part of the Highland Brigade and we were to
take orders from no one but him. It was the first time I'd
met the man and I found him quite charming. Of course, I
knew a lot about him already. He was a crofter's son from
Dingwall who had joined the army as a private soldier and
gradually worked up the ranks to become the hero he was
now. He was also a Gaelic speaker, which endeared him to
the men.

That same day, he had received a parcel of knitted socks,
sweets and our favourite tobacco, Golden Bar, from the
Glen Etive School, for distribution solely amongst
MacDonalds. I had eleven of the clan out of the hundred or
so men under my command and they were all delighted to
receive the gifts.

The general warned us that the Boer were changing their
tactics. The formal war had already been won by the
British, but now the Boer Commando were travelling without cumbersome wagons. They took only food, a blanket
and weapons. They would attack strung-out convoys, or
hold the high ground in a pass with their Maxim machine
guns, but then as soon as things got too hot for them, they
would vanish, only to reappear somewhere else. He fore-
saw that this new strategy would make things very difficult
for us. A mere hundred Boer would be able to harry a
brigade of several thousand and potentially inflict tremendous casualties. The general also observed that the Lovat
Scouts were the only regiment he knew of that was suited
to this new type of warfare.

In the preceding few weeks, there had been a spate of night attacks. The Boer had crept into British army camps at night, stolen weapons and cut the horses free. There was even an attack in broad daylight when twenty Boer, dressed in khaki and wearing British helmets, came riding up to a small convoy. With almost all our men now heavily bearded, it was impossible to tell they weren't British until they were right amongst our troops. Without a shot being fired, they captured two wagons of ammunition, one of food supplies and took all the horses.

The general had heard about the skills of Chief Scout Burnham and he was sceptical, until, with Blundell present, I told him of our experiences. Once, on a week-long patrol, our horses were growing weaker and thirstier as waterhole after waterhole we came across was dried up or polluted by the Boer dumping rotting animal carcasses into them. Burnham had taught us how to use sticks as water diviners so we were able to find a spring only a couple of feet under the ground in a nearby hollow. And in another instance, due to Burnham's instruction, we followed the tracks of a Boer Commando unit which had swept around in a circle and would have ambushed us if we hadn't spotted their spoor. Blundell wrote down my every word on the man, and his subsequent article about Burnham resulted in many follow-up pieces in the press.

General Kitchener's controversial instigation of the clearing of Boer families from their land – what was known as the scorched-earth policy – was also discussed. After agreeing with Blundell that the conversation be off the record, we expressed our doubts that this policy would actually bring the Boer men to heel. Blundell was of the opinion that the more the public got to hear of the appalling death rates in the camps, the greater would be the backlash against the war. It could only be damaging to the army's reputation. I agreed; this was a distasteful aspect and my men were keen to avoid it.

The general confided in us that he, too, thought the clearance policy was ill advised and that he was ashamed of it. 'Kitchener will live to regret it,' I recall him saying, before he showed us a letter he had received from a Boer corporal.

(Cprl) C. R. Van Niekerk,
Burgersdorp Commando,
O.F.S. Army

30th June 1900

General 'Fighting Mac'!

Sir, I beg to state that having been on commando for less than a year now, fighting a clean war and being civilised to your injured, I now have cause to be upset.

I understand that we are at war, but is it right that you now fight women and children? My wife and her six children were put out of their home and had to watch your 'gallant women-fighters' burn it to the ground. They were taken to the concentration camp at Bloemfontein. There, four of our children have died in two weeks.

Have my fellow Boer done anything similar to your side? They have not.

My men now want to go to the Cape Colony and burn down houses, and there is a lot of bitterness. Lots of our men will want to do this in the future. Is this what Kitchener and you call war?

The Boer people ask you to fight like gentlemen.

I have the honour to be, Sir, your obedient servant,

C. R. Van Niekerk

We knew the Boer were running out of ammunition. Their Long Tom field guns had been out of use for a while and their other artillery, too. Increasingly, they were coming after our .303s and ammunition. I told the general of one unfortunate young English officer and his men, who were caught by the Boer. After surrendering, their rifles, ammunition, horses and even their boots were taken, and he and his fifty cavalrymen had an ignominious day's walk into Aliwal North camp where they were greeted with much laughter by the garrison.

Blundell wanted information from MacDonald about the National Scouts, and the general was happy to tell him what he knew. He explained that Boer soldiers were offered inducements to come over to the British side, to work both as spies and in an active fighting unit called the National Scouts. To date, over five thousand men had switched. There was a deep antagonism between the Boer fighting against each other, with many instances of brother fighting brother. Those in the pay of the British were known as Judas-Boer or *hendsuppers*, and when captured by their brethren, they were paraded down the street and spat at by the women before being executed. MacDonald had heard that Kruger had a man whose job was to compile a list of those in the pay of the British. Kruger planned to have branding irons made in the shape of a cross so that after the war these men would be identified by the brands between the eyes.

There were dozens of men fighting for the Boer Commando with Scottish names like Maclean, Grant and MacDonald. When captured, they were treated exactly the same as the Boer prisoners, with no retribution. That said, we had heard of some atrocities from our side, too. After one night attack in Natal half a dozen Boer had been captured, lined up and shot by a firing squad.

The general was full of news that we junior officers normally didn't get to hear about, and Blundell obtained excellent copy for his newspaper. He told us that shortly after Christiaan de Wet, the Boer commander in chief, had captured a huge amount of ammunition and supplies at Rooiwal, his brother Piet, also a Boer general, had surrendered and was now fighting for the British. Christiaan had apparently remarked that he would shoot his brother if he ever laid eyes on him again.

A few weeks later, I found myself describing that dinner with Fighting Mac to Major Murray. We discussed the concentration camps and Kitchener's policy of herding Boer families together under British Army command. Initially the Boer had been in favour of the camps. It had only been twenty years since the Anglo-Zulu war, and there was a real concern that the black population would take the opportunity of the men being away on commando duties to seize the farms and capture, or even kill, the families. So, the women and children being corralled together, fed and kept safe was certainly preferable. However, as time went on, with farms being razed and the terrible conditions in the camps becoming widely known, an outcry went up about the inhumane treatment.

Donald John is my eyes and ears within the regiment. He has told me of ignorant men drinking water without boiling it, and of a man who received a distressing letter from home who needed my help. It was Donald John who told me how much unease there was amongst the men about the farm clearances and how some were saying they would refuse to be involved. I found it hard to believe the wild rumours of massive deaths in the camps: surely our side was better than this?

Chapter 13

Captain Willie MacDonald, South Africa, 1900

It was not long after Heilbron that Number Two Squadron caught up with us and Simon Lovat became well enough to rejoin as Number One squadron commander. I reverted to adjutant. I suspect they were rather envious when they learned the full facts about our relieving Heilbron and the high esteem in which we were now held.

After a relatively peaceful period, a move to seize control of the land to the south of Bethlehem and catch a key Boer force before they escaped into the mountains of Basutoland was afoot. The Afrikaners held a hilly area called the Vaal Krantz ridge, with a pass through it called Retiefs Nek. It was bitterly cold, with a strong wind and snow on the uplands. The Boer must have believed there was no chance of a night attack in such foul weather so they had moved down to the shelter and campfires of the veld below. But they had underestimated how well our Highland men thrive in these conditions. Once the Scouts and Highland Light Infantry had possession of the ridge, then the battle was won and our men controlled the pass.

It remained a constant battle though. We were sniped at incessantly. Private Barron was shot through the heart and

Lieutenant Brodie was hit in his left leg; it took four hours for our men to carry Brodie out after dark. We had heard what excellent marksmen the Boer farmers were, yet I cannot testify to that. About two hundred and fifty of them were concealed in the rocks a good four hundred yards from us, and all day they shot at us, and we at them. We sustained only one casualty but knew for certain that over thirty of them were killed by the Scouts. By now, Donald John had learned a lot of Dutch and his fluency had come in very useful. He overheard the Boer commandant shout to his men on the left to drop back and then come around behind our right flank. As a result, I sent half a dozen men back with the Maxim machine gun and they shot them all. We had one hundred and fifty bullets each and had completely run out by the time the enemy had cleared off.

I had never heard such a din. We had six or eight of our siege guns along with a naval gun and pom-poms, all mixed with the rat-a-tat-tat of machine guns and rifles. The Boer were incredibly brave to hold their position despite the rocks exploding around them. When the artillery was called off, the Camerons and Seaforths charged the Boer position, with the burghers running and tumbling down the hill in their rush to get away.

On 30 July 1900, I wrote to my mother.

Bethlehem, O.F.S.

Dearest Mother,

I am writing this while sitting on top of a *kopje*, waiting for fighting to begin. We left Bethlehem in a great hurry nine days ago and have been fighting every day since then. We had a two-day fight at Retiefs Nek, a narrow pass into the hills held by six thousand Boer. Our first night there was dismal – heavy rain, followed by snow showers and sleet. This was our preparation for battle. I woke up with two inches of water under my bed which was a real joy! In the morning, our big guns shelled while the Black Watch, Highland Light Infantry and Sussex attacked the ridge.

The Black Watch got up pretty well on the left but the Highland Light Infantry were held back by the steep rocks. The Sussex were beaten back on the right. This took all day. At night we offered to go along the ridge under cover of darkness and command the pass at daylight, but Hector would not allow it so instead we sent Sergeant Dewar, Dugald MacDonald and John McDonald the Boss up to reconnoitre the ground. They found two seemingly uninhabited Boer camps, with fires and camps two thousand feet below. Then they returned and woke the colonel at 3.30 a.m. to take his men, plus our two hundred Scouts along the ridge. Dugald and Dewar showed them the way. We got to the pass ten minutes before the Boer began to come up from their side, and after two hours we had secured the pass. We fought hard on the left and charged a *kopje* with the Seaforth and had some fine shooting at the Boer, who were streaming across the plain below. This finished the fight and we returned to camp. General Hunter sent for Lovat the next day and made four points:

1) The Lovat Scouts had done considerably more than their share in the two days;

2) It was thanks to the three Scouts that the ridge was won, and it was this that gained the day;

3) The stalking glass was astoundingly useful with a good man behind it;

4) A special message would be sent to Lord Roberts as to the conduct of the Scouts.

Hunter parted company with our force that day but kept six of the Scouts with him. And our gallant three, two of whom were Lochaber men, were mentioned in dispatches.

Your ever loving son,

W. MacDonald

I was afraid that I would not be able to settle down after the war as the excitement of the action had become so intoxicating. Days would pass without my thinking about Jack and his struggles with the whisky business; it seemed distant and unimportant when my immediate concern was keeping my men and myself alive.

The next day, Sergeant Major MacNeil, Donald John, General MacDonald and I spied from a hilltop the Boer Commando below. We observed thousands of men, several hundred wagons and a valley full of livestock. We had them surrounded. Within two days, the general surrendered his six thousand men. We didn't really know what was happening elsewhere, but I couldn't help but think that this would finish the show and we would be sent home in six weeks.

That night, there was a grand supper for the men, with an issue of rum, a visit by our own general and congratulatory speeches by Murray and Simon. Hector told us that he was immensely proud of us and did not forget to say so to everybody. It was during the dinner that Sergeant Cameron – newly released – arrived. He just strolled in and took his measure of rum, to wild applause from everyone. He had been with the Boer for six weeks, and when they surrendered, he and half a dozen other prisoners had been released. The Scouts were just like a family, an extraordinarily tight group of men, and it made one fiercely proud.

Immediately after the surrender, the Boer were stripped of their guns and horses. The encampment was surrounded by troops, then a couple of days later, a two-mile-long line of men was walked, over the course of two days, towards Bethlehem. There, they were put on trains to take them south. With such a major engagement won and the capture of so many badly needed, and excellent horses to boot, the Imperial forces had taken a significant step forwards.

Chapter 14

Captain Willie MacDonald, South Africa, 1900

The days that followed passed slowly; the dejected Dutch shuffled along, in no hurry to be sent off to the colonies for the rest of the war. During this trek I rode alongside Sergeant Cameron and took the opportunity to ask him about his family – his father Ewan in particular. My father had described him as 'a colourful and affectionate rogue' and said there were more stories about this man than any other in Lochaber. His son, however, loyally insisted that he was now quite an old fellow, living quietly near Achnacarry. Yet, as we rode, the stories tumbled out.

The family hailed originally from Glen Dessary at the top of Loch Arkaig. His father had been the biggest distiller of illegal whisky in the west, Cammy believed. Their still was located at the old Hanoverian barracks, from where they transported the whisky by pony to the west via Camusrory, over Bonnie Prince Charlie's route or Glenfinnan or down the loch to Achnacarry Castle and out that way. The excise men, or 'gaugers' as he called them, couldn't get near there without being seen by the locals, who knew well that they would be handsomely rewarded by Ewan for getting the news to him of a raid.

The gaugers knew there was illegal *uisge beatha* being distilled in the area and were determined to make a catch. Meanwhile, Ewan had a big order of whisky to go to Edinburgh. He heard that the gaugers had set up an ambush by the bridge over the Caledonian Canal at Gairlochy, but as luck would have it, the old Cameron chief had recently passed away and his funeral cortege would be going over that bridge on a certain date in early December. Sensing an opportunity, Ewan ordered the smartest carriage available from Fort William a day early, and arranged that the two carriage attendants would be kitted out in funeral attire, complete with top hats and frock coats.

The flagons of whisky were transported down the loch at dawn, and loaded onto the carriage, in the luggage trunks on the back and under the seats. Ewan and his man 'borrowed' the hats and frock coats from the Fort William men, moved off down to the castle, and took some of the Lochiel party on board. As the funeral party proceeded over the canal, the gaugers were there, all lined up, hats held to their chests in respect to the dead chief. The rendez-vous with the Edinburgh smuggler and his ponies took place at Corriechoillie that evening, after which the whisky was taken along the old drove road and on to the south.

The sergeant told me this tale knowing that I was from a whisky family myself. I took great pleasure in recounting it to my friend, Donald the Younger of Lochiel, when we met up with the 51st at Bloemfontein a month or two later. He had never heard it before and was highly amused. During times like these with Sergeant Cameron, I often felt the urge to talk about the family business and its problems, but I knew I had to bite my tongue. He would not be able to resist writing home about our conversation and the news would be all over Lochaber. Donald John, on the other hand, could be counted upon to be discreet.

We rode thirty-five miles north to Lindley, where we recuperated and waited for fresh clothes and mounts for several days. On the trek there, we twice came across areas strewn with the putrefying carcasses of horses and oxen; you could smell them long before you could see them. There was also a sprinkling of khaki army stores, some smashed-up wagons and piled-up stones marking recently dug graves. Vultures flapped into the air as we approached and jackals circled nearby, waiting for our troop to pass. After a scrap, the Boer would always come by to take what they needed; they, too, needed boots and clothing.

There was a critical shortage of horses, reportedly around ten thousand across the army, despite those taken by us after Retiefs Nek. So many had died in battle, and not only through combat; the poor beasts succumbed to disease, broken limbs and snake bites. Our new mounts, given to us in Lindley, turned out to be in almost as bad a condition as the old, with some suffering from strangles and mange. We all competed to get one of the captured Boer horses rather than the untrained and skittish Argentinian animals that had recently arrived. Fresh clothes were desperately needed, too; our breeches were in tatters, shabby and full of holes. I confess thinking that Donald John looked quite indecent when seen from behind.

We loved receiving post. The camp would fall silent for an entire afternoon as letters and newspapers – the

Inverness Courier and *Oban Times* – were read and re-read.
There was much consternation at a letter published in the
Courier, which had been forwarded by an anxious mother,
complaining of the poor food and how the Scouts were
always given the dangerous jobs. Lovat immediately sat
down to pen a reply rebutting the complaint. Quite a few
of the men were unable to read or write, but that evening,
pairs of men were seen throughout the camp composing
their replies home.

My brother Jack had written – a curt, angry letter in
which he accused me of being selfish because I had decided
to remain in South Africa. He raged that there were
hundreds of thousands of soldiers in the Imperial Army out
here, and how could my role be *that* important? He reiter-
ated how my help would be crucial to him. I wrote back
straight away, saying that now was not the time: it was
believed that with Pretoria fallen, one more big push would
win the war and then, with our mission accomplished, the
volunteer regiments would be the first sent home.

We heard that President Kruger had fled from Pretoria
with over a million pounds of state funds. Many of the Boer
fighters considered this an abdication of the presidency, and
there was rumoured to be considerable dissent amongst
them. 'Oom Paul', Uncle Paul, as the Boer affectionately
named Kruger, had proposed that the Boer should negotiate
peace, which Steyn, the President of the Orange Free State,
had rejected. We also heard through the rumour mill that
Kruger was to be replaced by General Botha as president.

One morning, General MacDonald summoned me. He
needed an important document taken to Lord Roberts,
who was based to the east of Johannesburg at

Witwatersrand. I had to be back within a week with his response. With only Donald John to accompany me, we set off immediately on the three hundred-mile return journey on fresh, fast horses. We aimed to cover forty miles a day but managed to do more than that, camping at Frankfort on the first night and Bethal on the second. The only Boer we saw were at a distance. They fired a few random shots at us but didn't attempt to give chase. It was a comfort to be in a town each night, where there was a safe garrison and food for ourselves and the horses.

When we arrived at our destination, Lord Roberts and the High Commissioner were in a meeting with the mining magnates Cecil Rhodes and his partner Charles Rudd, along with Alfred Beit and Julius Wernher, two London magnates who dominated the finances of the Rand mining houses. I was aware that there was British pressure for De Beers and the Anglo Gold Mines and their financiers to make a significant contribution to the war. As we waited for the meeting to conclude, it was Donald John who made the connection: Rudd had bought Ardnamurchan Estate a few years ago and was rebuilding the old inn at Shiel Bridge as his main house. He had made his fortune from diamonds and gold, and was believed to be one of the richest men in the world. Donald John had seen the new house from the road not long before he came out.

It was a popular opinion that the real reason for the war was that the British wanted to wrest control of the goldfields of Witwatersrand from the Boer, in the knowledge that they would be as lucrative as the diamond mines at Kimberley had been. And there was another big issue that the High Commissioner wanted to resolve: votes in the north were restricted to those of Dutch extraction, and neither the black South Africans nor the hundreds of thousands of white incomers – known as *uitlanders* – were entitled to vote.

The meeting eventually ended, and Lord Roberts' aide invited me into the room. General MacDonald was talking to a tall, thin man with a long black beard, Boer-style. Lord Roberts greeted me warmly – he'd heard of me from General Hector after the relief of Heilbron – and I presented the document to him. He opened it and started reading while the other man introduced himself to me as Charles Rudd. I told him I was a Lochaber man, who lived within a day's ride from his place at Shiel Bridge, which took him by surprise.

That evening, I dined with those involved in the discussions as Charles Rudd's guest. It was a magnificent meal: four courses accompanied by champagne and the finest French wine. Rudd travelled with a chef who, he said proudly, used to work at Claridge's. He told me that his house at Shiel Bridge had burned down just as he had been ready to move in and that he had recently remarried following the death of his previous wife. They had ambitious plans for the estate. He wondered whether to rebuild Shiel Bridge at all as he was now building a castle at Glenborrodale and many other estate houses. He insisted I come to visit him in Argyll, which I promised to do. He was clearly ready to retire and to live there permanently.

As we set off at first light the following morning, I reflected on this meeting. Rudd didn't seem to know people on the west coast, and I think he was as pleased about our introduction as I was. I declared to Donald John that I would certainly call on him, not least because I'd never dined so well in my life the night before.

Chapter 15

Donald John, South Africa, 1901

We had been in the veld since May. The cold dry winter was over, and summer, around British New Year time, was as hot as hell down there. We were now in constant engagement with the enemy. The Boer were playing hide and seek – twenty men here, a hundred there – and would snipe at us from the hills, attack at night and blow up ammunition stores and stationary trains.

It was especially difficult for our infantry and artillery; the Boer were so mobile on their horses, our men were struggling to fight back. The Scouts would be sent on three-day reconnoitres to a hamlet or pass where the enemy had been seen and would frequently be greeted by nothing but the embers of a warm fire. Once, however, we came tantalisingly close, finding their dinner still cooking on the fire but no sign of human life. Our hungry men made short work of the delicious mutton, mealies and pomegranates.

In a letter home I tried to explain a typical engagement with the Boer. The Highland Brigade would move from one town to another in a massive convoy of three thousand infantry – the Black Watch, Seaforths, Argylls and more

– all marching in their separate battalions. Fighting Mac had around fifty mounted men and a couple of carts allocated to him. Then there would be the supply wagons pulled by ten oxen and at least thirty others spread between the infantry battalions. These would be the most vulnerable to attack, and being loaded with ammunition and food supplies, they were much sought after by the Boer. There would be about three hundred black Africans, hired to look after the supplies, and peripheral support personnel such as vets, doctors, carters and a blacksmith all with their own carts, mules and horses.

In the event of a broken wheel or axle, the entire convoy would have to stop while it was repaired, or else the wagon emptied and abandoned. Slowest of all were the sheep or cattle which might have been requisitioned – our food for the week ahead. At least a dozen dogs would be darting around, seemingly without owners, foraging for meat from the dead horses that we sometimes came across. The convoy could be up to three miles long and it crawled along at a frustrating two miles an hour. The Lovat Scouts and a unit of African mounted troops had the role of outliers ahead, behind and on the flanks, looking out for raiding Boer parties who often dashed in and seized supplies from a lagging wagon, or galloped alongside, firing at random into the dense units of men.

The number of Scouts available for active service had almost halved by this time as forty of our men had gone off to join the police, and we were suffering terribly from sickness, so there was talk of merging the two companies into one. Meanwhile, General Baden-Powell, we heard, was having huge arguments with everyone. General MacDonald had apparently told Lord Lovat that Baden-Powell was the most hated man in South Africa and had made a very bad start for the police by quarrelling with both High Commissioner Milner and Kitchener. He had also rejected the Lovat Scouts for being too untidy and unruly when they arrived for duty, and Lord Lovat had had to go to Pretoria where he successfully interceded on their behalf. That evening he gave our men a splendid farewell dinner, by all accounts.

Being outliers for the Highland Brigade was energetic, exciting work, but on rare occasions we were given the more mundane job of protecting a supply convoy as it crept up-country; we Scouts considered this task very much beneath us. On the other hand, when there was a downpour on the veld, it could turn this tedious task into an enormous challenge. One time we went to Philippolis – a very pretty place when the sun was out – to help with a huge convoy of ammunition, clothing and food heading north towards Johannesburg. We were travelling in constant heavy rain and in two days managed less than five miles. At times, even forty powerful oxen couldn't pull a wagon, the mud was so deep. Everyone was exhausted. Another time, when we were taking a crucial convoy across the Caledon river, swollen after rainfall, the officers' mess wagon – the first across – tipped over. It was a hell of a job to right it, and as a result, it was decided that a drift would have to be dug to make a crossing point. With the banks forty feet high, this proved an enormous task, and there were more than a hundred men with shovels on each side, digging for two days solid. Everyone was caked in red mud. Then, thirty oxen, pulling an ammunition wagon, came to a halt in the middle of the river. The Africans were standing on the backs of the oxen, completely naked, cracking their whips and shouting like madmen. The Seaforths had to cross the river holding onto a rope, their kilts above their necks. Somehow we made it over without serious mishap. It took twelve hours, with only one death: a drowned ox. It was an extraordinary experience – one I'll never forget.

There was much talk in the camp when Queen Victoria died. The newspapers from home contained photographs of her grand funeral procession. I was asked to play the pipes at a ceremony to commemorate the passing of the old and in with the new at a parade, where Major Murray called out, 'God bless Queen Victoria, God bless the King, King Edward.' We all raised our hats. We were cheered by the announcement from our new queen, Alexandra, that she would raise a nursing corps for the South Africa Campaign.

When we first arrived in South Africa, there was a policy for dealing with captured Boer fighters: on surrender of their rifle they received ten pounds. They handed over their Mausers and went home to their families for a month. It took several months for our generals to realise that: one, they didn't have ammunition for the surrendered Mausers anyway, and two, after their family holiday, the men would just join up again – this time, armed with a captured British rifle.

The policy was swiftly changed: the captured men were sent abroad to camps in St Helena, the island where we stopped on the ship coming down, and also in Ceylon and India.

Lieutenant Kenny Macdonald finally rejoined us. Although he had recovered from his illness, he was horribly gaunt, and he had grown a beard which he trimmed to a point, like a Yankee. We all had full beards by then. I was startled when I caught sight of myself in the mirror at the company stores wagon – my beard was completely white yet the hair on my head remained red. Morag would not have appreciated my new look. On previous occasions when I'd tried to grow a beard, she'd always kept me at a distance until I shaved it off. We looked very like the Boer fighters by then, although they usually wore white shirts underneath their jackets and cartridge belts over the shoulder, whereas we wore khaki shirts and belts around our waist.

We were camped at Lindley, south of Johannesburg, and John MacDonald the Boss went out alone one day to scout a *kopje*. He ran into five Boer, who called on him to surrender. He proceeded to shoot one and turned to flee, but his horse was shot, and so, scrambling off the animal, he threw himself down a slope, tumbling as shots rained down upon him. He was found by three of our men a couple of hours later, battered and bruised but otherwise in good shape. He was back on a horse and ready for action the next morning.

I enjoyed being on patrol with Cammy. A Lochielside man, he'd done well in the Camerons before getting a job on Lochiel Estates. We had come to know each other through selling sheep at the auction mart in the Fort, and when Captain MacDonald was recruiting, he was an obvious choice. We were a bit unusual, the two of us. We were older than the other Scouts, in fact old enough to be the fathers of some, but I believe our similar ages brought us closer together.

When he had wandered into our camp, having been
freed after the Boer surrender at Retiefs Nek, it was as if he
had been away seeing friends. He was a cool character if
ever there was one – someone you'd want at your back in
a fight. With him was his old friend Archie Macdonald, the
Glencoe man from the Lord Strathcona's Horse we'd met
briefly at the Cape when we disembarked. Archie had been
captured at Standerton fighting as part of General Buller's
force.

During one of our patrols, as we rode side by side,
Cammy told me about his time as a Boer prisoner and how
he'd used Burnham's advice about knowing your enemy.
'You couldn't meet a nicer group of men than the Boer,' he
said. 'They fought hard but would do anything to help the
injured. Most spoke English. Of course, they'd fought
alongside the British twenty years before. In fact, I met two
or three who were from England and had only been in
South Africa for a few years. One became a friend. He
explained to me that the two of them had joined the Boer
because the British had ridden into their farms and taken
their horses and cattle. What else could they do but join
up?

'There was such a strong feeling of injustice about how
General Kitchener was behaving towards the Boer families,'
he continued. 'Do you know, Donald John, Afrikaners
wouldn't bite into their husks without offering you half?
And they treat their horses far better than our Tommies do
theirs. Great riders, they can stay in the saddle for twenty-
four hours at a time. They're heartily fed up with the war
but I know they'll fight on. They'll never surrender.'

I agreed.

'Mind you, I was shocked at how they treated black people – rougher than they did their horses. Men would get whipped if they were lazy and they were fed half what the white men got. On no account would they be given rifles as there was considerable fear that they would rebel. Milner's proposal to give the black population the vote after the war was another reason why the Boer were ready to fight to the end.'

'So there's a way to go yet?'

Cammy nodded. 'There was a council of Boer generals, where they decided to change their way of fighting. Those big forces of men with artillery and wagons would be replaced by fast-moving commando units who knew the local land, who could lie up during the day and attack at night. Food and ammunition would come from the British they attacked. Every British convoy would be harried by snipers from a distance and the railway tracks and bridges blown up.'

'This is pretty much what Fighting Mac told my boss would happen,' I said. 'We're already seeing just that, aren't we?'

We rode on in silence for a while until Cammy changed the subject.

He told me about Archie Macdonald, who was with the Canadian army. Lord Strathcona had personally raised and paid for five hundred and fifty men to be trained and shipped to Cape Town. The majority were country lads from the north-west, cattle men or lumberjacks, as well as a few Mounties. The Canadians talked fondly about the Rockies: the dramatic twelve thousand-foot-high mountains, the enormous trees, the wild bears, the twenty feet of snow in the winter and sweltering heat in the summer. It all sounded such a different and exciting world to Cammy. Archie himself now lived in Cape Breton, Nova Scotia, in a village called Glencoe. He had been brought up in Glencoe in Argyll and had family there still. Lord Strathcona had made his money building the Canadian Pacific Railway. He'd bought Glencoe Estate in Scotland, and Archie's brother worked for him. It was because of all these Glencoe connections that Archie had been selected.

Cammy planned to head out to Cape Breton with his wife when the war was over. Archie had promised to set him up. There was land available and he would have his own farm rather than being a shepherd at the laird's bidding.

He looked across at me with a grin. 'You and Morag and the family should come, too!'

I shook my head. 'You know me better than that, Cammy,' I replied. 'I'll live and die at Peanmeanach.'

Chapter 16

Donald John, Ardnish, 1944

I feel as though this coughing fit will finish me off. I can scarcely catch my breath, and I can see the alarm in Louise's face as she rubs my back. She keeps asking me if I'm all right and telling me to breathe normally, that it will pass. She has the professional air of the nurse she was. Mairi brings me water to sip but I splutter and spit it out, unable to swallow.

When the coughing finally eases, my ribs ache and every breath causes sharp pain. But I lie still and say nothing of it. I can sense their distress at their helplessness. I close my eyes and we all sit in a silence only broken by the gentle hiss of the peat and the howl of the wind.

Eventually, Louise speaks. I can hear the effort she's putting into making her voice light and carefree. 'Angus, do you enjoy being a priest? Why don't you tell us what led you to the priesthood? It's been such a long time since we spoke of it.'

I smile at her thoughtfulness in allowing me to rest quietly and listen. Opening my eyes, I watch my son, who has straightened up in his chair and seems to be collecting his thoughts.

'Very well,' he says, 'though I'm not sure where to begin. Maybe it was our connection with Father Allan MacDonald from South Uist. Father knew him from his early days in Fort William, didn't you?' I nod. 'And, Mairi, weren't your family good friends of his in Eriskay?'

'A fine man,' she says cheerfully.

'He came here to stay twice when I was a young teenager. He was a cousin of the Archbishop and I thought he was a great man, an inspirational priest. We had such long, interesting chats when I was staying with the Archbishop's mother in the Fort. I was going to Mass the whole time and was inspired by the nuns' teaching at the school. I don't remember a distinct calling from God or anything like that, though; it was more of a steady drift towards my decision, which didn't seem that momentous at the time.'

I shake my head in amusement. 'Come, Angus, there's more to it than that, I can tell.'

I see his face flush. 'Well, of course there is,' he stammers, 'but it's a long story.'

'Do we not have all evening?' Louise smiles and glances over at me. 'What say you, Father? Would you like to hear tell of your son's journey all the way from Peanmeanach to the priesthood?'

I feel a lump in my throat, and nod. There is nothing I would like more.

Angus, too, seems emotional as he continues. 'I'm afraid I was like all young men, wanting to make my own way in life and not wanting my parents ordering me about like I was a child.'

He looks at me. 'Father, I'm so sorry about all the arguments. I know you were having difficult times; you were just back from the war and had just lost your leg …' He pauses, before adding, 'I was an awkward lad.'

I wave away his apology. 'No need for that, son, no need at all,' I whisper. 'Go on with your story.'

He smiles. 'Very well. I was restless, I admit to that, although I was sad going off, leaving Sheena and Donald Peter at home. I always tried to get home for a couple of weeks a year to help with the hay and the potatoes. Before I went, you were always asking if I had a girl on the go and when would I get a proper job at the aluminium smelter or one of the estates. I just got a bit fed up of being nagged. Anyhow, Captain Willie came to my rescue, if you recall. I left with him to go to Fort William.

'I headed off to work for Charles Rudd at Ardnamurchan Estate first of all. I think you met him in South Africa, didn't you, Father? Captain Willie said he'd try to get me a position on the estate, and that's how it turned out. We set off on horseback, took the ferry across the narrows at Corran and stayed at the Maclean of Ardgour's house. I was in the servants' quarters, obviously, but I was treated very well. Then we had a long ride to Glenborrodale Castle, which was a magnificent building of red stone. My goodness, I'd never seen such grandeur: the uniformed servants, the fancy Panhard car on the drive and the lovely yacht, *Mingary*, moored in the bay.

'It was bewildering at first. The building was so new there was still furniture arriving and constant deliveries. Business guests were coming and going. Our horses were led off and I was taken to meet the house staff at supper. The servants ate like royalty, it seemed to me, and the next morning I was delighted to be offered a job as the laird's piper until October that year when Rudd was due to sail back to tend to his business affairs in South Africa.

'The butler fitted me out with a kilt, doublet and glengarry, and told to me wear this the whole time – except when I was sleeping!

'I travelled everywhere with the laird and his young wife, in his carriage to Shiel Bridge, and in his yacht to Inveraray Castle and Bute. At the castle my duties were to pipe the household out of bed at seven thirty with a reveille, pipe them on and off the *Mingary*, and pipe the guests in to dinner. Apart from a wedding or funeral amongst the community, that was that. It was an easy role and it earned me a handsome pay packet. In my spare time I ran to get fit and worked on my piping. I had a plan for my future.

'It was a wonderful experience, but there were two problems. The first was the butler. He was a tough South African called Jacob Baak who seemed to have it in for me . . .' He frowned.

'And the second?' Louise presses.

'We were banned from speaking Gaelic,' he says, too quickly. 'Presumably because Baak didn't speak it and was worried about us talking behind his back. I seemed to be the culprit with everything, and was always put to washing the pots or taking the laird's dogs for a walk before bed.'

'And why might that have been?' I ask, enjoying making mischief.

Angus sighs. 'Oh, all right. The second problem wasn't really the Gaelic. It was Corrie.'

'Corrie? Who was that?' Louise asks, wide-eyed.

'Rudd's wife,' Angus admits. 'She was the same age as me and less than half that of her husband. She was recently over from South Africa and everything was new to her. Tanned, fair-haired, tall and elegant, she was a . . . delight.'

'Goodness!' Louise exclaims. 'A real beauty!'

Angus sighs. 'Oh yes. And of course Rudd was always busy in meetings or out with the builders and estate workers. He was worried that she'd get bored, so I was asked to show her around. She wanted to learn to fish, so I took her up to the freshwater lochs and she would have a good few in her basket for the return. I taught her how to shoot with a rifle as she was keen to stalk deer when the season came along. Then I took her on a visit to an illegal whisky still that I knew of. I had to tie her scarf around her eyes so she wouldn't know of its location. I told her a little about Tearlach, Mother's cousin, who made whisky at an old nunnery on the island of Canna. He was always asking me to go and work there with him. He would bring the whisky over in big containers and bottle it at Rhu, just to the north of us, using second-hand Long John, Dewar's and White Horse bottles in order to smuggle it down to Glasgow.'

'So you spent a bit of time alone with her?' Louise enquires, eager to know more.

'I did, yes. And as the weeks passed, I confess I fell madly in love with her. I would find any excuse to be with her. She would follow the sound of my pipes down to the lochside and sit on the jetty listening while I played, as Baak watched from the castle. Another day I was practising my dancing for the Highland Games and she begged me to teach her. I was holding her around the waist to lift her, both of us laughing, when who should come in but Baak. Although nothing happened between us, it was an unfortunate coincidence how often Baak would come around the corner when Corrie was close to me.'

'No coincidence at all,' Mairi adds, winking at Louise.

'The last straw came when I was teaching her Gaelic. The two of us were sitting side by side in the dining room, a book between us on the table. Corrie was giggling as she tried to pronounce a difficult word, and I put my hand on hers – only for a second, mind. We looked up, and there stood Baak and Mr Rudd.'

'Oh no!' Louise clapped her hands to her face. 'What happened?'

'Within an hour I was walking down the road towards Salen in the clothes I'd arrived in, with no time for a farewell to Corrie or the other servants.'

'You poor thing, Angus,' Louise says. 'Where did you go?'

'I knew I'd have a bit of explaining to do to Captain Willie, and so three days later I presented myself at the Ben Nevis distillery, cap in hand. We had a cup of tea in his office and I told him of my being expelled in disgrace. I expected him to be furious with me, of course, but instead, he called in his brother Jack and got me to repeat the entire story. They just dissolved into fits of laughter whenever I imitated Baak's voice telling me off.'

Angus laughs softly at the recollection, then pauses. I see his shoulders slumping.

'Despite my laughter now, I was very sad about Corrie for a long time. Although she had given me no indication, I really felt she shared my love. I eventually decided to write a letter asking her to meet me in Fort William, but I never heard back. Perhaps Baak or her husband intercepted it. Anyway, as time passed I told myself she wouldn't be daft enough to exchange her rich husband for a kilted young crofter's son who could play a nice jig. It was likely just a holiday infatuation for her . . .'

'Go on, Angus, finish your story,' I urge him.

'Well, after I left Rudd's employment I spent the next three years doing piecemeal work here and there, but I always made myself available to compete at the Gatherings. With piping in my blood – thanks to you, Father – I wanted to have a good go at competing in the Highland Games. And I'd always been strong and fast so tossing the caber, throwing the hammer and the races were my ambition – and the prize money was well worth having. I boarded in luxury with Captain Willie's mother at Invernevis House in Fort William; she had a room at the back of the house that I could come and go from in exchange for doing some chores.

'Peter MacLennan had the General Store and I was the boy carrying boxes off the steamer and loading up the wagon, or carrying hundredweight bags of oats off the train and dividing them up for the customers. Sometimes I would get the early train to Corpach and work on the Caledonian Canal, opening and closing the locks at Neptune's Staircase and playing the pipes for the tourists. I earned a good few tips from the yachts coming through there.

'The harder the work, the happier I was, and I was getting paid to get myself in good shape for the Highland Games in the summer. There was a mine just opened in Strontian I thought about approaching, but it was too far away. Then I met a foreman of McAlpine's in the Volunteer

Arms – I knew him from the Mallaig railway work – and heard there was some well-paid work in Kinlochleven. He gave me a letter of introduction, and I walked over the hill by the General Wade road and stayed through a couple of the wettest months of the winter. My job was messenger for the foreman and I had to run back and forth for ten hours a day, from the village up to the site.

'It was as rough as hell over there, with thousands of men, mainly Irish navvies, employed to build the Blackwater Dam and the aluminium plant. Fights broke out every night, and the men were coarse, with language rougher than I'd ever heard. The work itself was terribly dangerous: men were dying the whole time, falling off the scaffolding or getting hit by machinery. I remember being appalled when I saw how many graves there were up by the dam.

'We slept in tents, and I'd wake in the same sodden clothes I'd worn the day before. There was porridge for breakfast, watery soup at midday and gravy of some description with a mountain of potatoes from the canteen in the evenings.

'A big woman called Kitty O'Leary ran the bar and sold her homemade potcheen in the centre of the town, and although the police knew fine it was there, they dared not try to close it down, for fear of a riot. The potcheen was cheap, vile and lethal. I shared a tent with a lad who was decent enough when sober, but a hell of a man for fighting when he was with the drink. On a Thursday and Friday night, his pay would go straight across to Kitty O'Leary, and by three in the morning he would come crashing into the tent with blood on his face, a broken nose or missing tooth – and more enemies made.

'One day he fell a hundred feet from the top of the dam, just yards from where I was standing. I went across to him and could see that he was dead. His body was smashed, his face frozen in terror. Looking up, I saw the men at the top looking down and I had no doubt they'd thrown him off. But I knew they would close ranks and there would be no prosecutions. The verdict was accidental death.'

'It sounds like you were in real danger there,' says Louise.

Angus nods. 'That was it. I fled back to Invernevis, and the luxury of a bath and the obligatory seven o'clock Mass at the convent every morning with Mrs MacDonald and the house staff. I told her that Kinlochleven was so rough that the postman had to have two policemen escort him in.

'Mrs MacDonald had a cook and a couple of girls in service. We used to go to dances together at the Banavie Hotel or for a drink at the Drover's Bar. One of the girls was from Barra and the other from Bohuntin. They had been at Invernevis for over a year and had lived a quiet life; they were shy girls and not used to big towns. We had fun together; I think they liked having a young man to take them out. Greta, the Barra girl, was married within a year and went to live in Invergarry, and Sophie became the cook for Captain Willie in Spean Bridge.

'At the Highland Games that summer I piped and danced and competed in all the adult men's track races. I even did the heavy events, too. I won almost seven pounds despite coming second in virtually everything! That was more than a working man would make in a year back then. I never won in the athletics as Ewen Mackenzie outran me every time, and on the heavies I was up against the legendary A.

A. Cameron, who was the world heavyweight champion. I won all the piping, though.'

I hear the pride in his voice and smile. 'We came to see you at the Lochaber Gathering at Jubilee Park,' I remind him, 'and there was that photograph of us with you in the *Oban Times*, laden down with cups and shields!'

He beams. 'I remember that day so well. Captain Willie had a party of guests there and amongst them were the Rudds. Corrie watched me all day.'

'Did you speak to her?' Louise asks.

'I did not, but I was proud she saw me.' His face reddens.

'What about the race up the Ben?' I ask, to help him out.

'Oh yes, that was the event everyone was talking about. There was to be a race up Ben Nevis and I trained hard for it, running up to the observatory and hotel at the top at eight o'clock every morning. Mr MacLennan gave me newspapers that came off the early train so the clientele at the hotel could read them at breakfast. I'd be back down by ten and off to work. I was lucky that all my employers knew of my sporting ambitions and allowed me the flexibility.

'Anyway, I took part in the first Ben race, but it was won, predictably, by Ewen Mackenzie. He worked on the path there so he was incredibly fit. The third year I did it, I took a bad tumble coming down and hurt my knee badly enough that I couldn't compete again in any races, so that was the end of my lucrative career at the Highland Gatherings.'

He looks up sheepishly. 'I think the story of my journey to the priesthood has meandered somewhat.'

'We're all enjoying it,' Louise reassures him.

'Well, it was my time at Invernevis that first got me thinking about becoming a priest. I couldn't continue competing,
and as time went on I began to feel unfulfilled.'

'And you realised Corrie would never be yours?' Louise
says gently.

He shrugs. 'Perhaps. I don't know. But throughout everything the Church has always been important to the family
and it still fascinates me. Remember when the Archbishop
was ordained at Fort Augustus Abbey? He came to stay
with his mother while I was there and we had these endless
talks about God into the early hours. I was intrigued. It
was then, one autumn day, when he and I went to see his
brother Captain Willie at Blarour in Spean Bridge. There
was a golf course, and as we struggled round, for some
reason I made up my mind. I went off to the seminary at
the Scots College in Rome shortly after and the Archbishop
has been my mentor ever since.'

'I was so proud at your ordination in Glasgow,' I say.
'The Archbishop himself was on the altar. What a day that
was!'

'And what a party back here afterwards!' Angus adds.

I close my eyes again, content and ready for sleep.

Chapter 17

Captain Willie MacDonald, South Africa, 1901

At Aliwal North, where the Orange Free State garrison was, we had a hut which served as the officers' mess, an improvement on the canvas sail strung between two wagons that made do while we were on trek. The food was good, although rations had to be expensively supplemented by purchases of milk, bread and fresh meat whenever they could be had. My mess bill worked out at about one pound and nine shillings every fortnight.

There were sulphur springs which had been turned into a bathhouse in the town, and we also had access to the Royal Hotel, which we treated rather like a club, a place to write letters and meet officers from other regiments.

Despite these welcome comforts, the men were ready to go home, myself as much as the next man. My brother's letters were growing increasingly desperate and I was concerned for him. We had all signed up as volunteers and had been there almost a year. Lovat had been sent home to raise a Second Contingent and we were told that we could go as soon as they arrived to replace us. General Hector MacDonald had been sent to India. He thought very highly of us and made his views know to the other generals before his departure. But that said, we felt considerable unease at the fact that our champion had left us.

We heard news of a farm being burned down nearby; British troops had caught a Boer man and were beating him hard. Lieutenant Grant went out to have a try for him but was too late. Strong winds had fanned the flames across the veld and a huge tranche of land had caught fire. There was nothing anyone could do except gallop ahead and see if there were convoys or others in its course. The night sky was lit up by the flames, with gum trees flaring a good hundred feet into the air and exploding like fireworks. Gazelles and other wild beasts scattered to safety. The fire only stopped when it reached a river.

In early June one of our messengers arrived with the news that there was a large Boer gathering near Burgersdorp. I told him that if he could get me on a hill within half a mile of them without being seen, I'd give him a guinea. Donald John, the messenger and I headed off.

It was a typical African winter morning, cool and dry with low, rolling mist on the distant hills, rather like a pleasant spring morning at home. The messenger knew the area well and we covered the ground quickly until we got into the hills. There, the thorn bushes were impenetrable and our horses refused go any further. It would be dark within the hour, so my plan was to creep up as close as we could on foot. When daylight came, we would have a good view down into the valley, assuming there were no sentries on the *kopje*. We tethered the horses and set off.

In case there were observers on the hill, we did just as you would do stalking a deer: one man spied the hill with his glass and the others crawled forward, then another would take out his glass while the others moved ahead. We were soon safely in position.

The Boer had a well-hidden camp, deep in the bush and surrounded by hills. In the dusk we had a clear view down onto the campfires below. The next morning, as the sun rose, we could see everything. We estimated there must have been a thousand men or more, and they weren't preparing to leave. 'This could be one of the decisive moments of the war,' I whispered to Donald John as I drew a sketch of everything I could see, marking where they had sentries. We calculated that if we could get four battalions of men to block each of the four exit routes then we would have them trapped. Surrender would surely follow.

We scurried back the way we had come and by mid-afternoon were back in camp reporting to Brigade Commander Colonel Gorringe. I told him and the other assembled commanding officers of my plan, showed them my sketches and proposed a strategy. Gorringe was notoriously rude and unpleasant, and was known as 'Bloody Orange' throughout the army. However, that day, he shook me by the hand and told everyone what a sound officer I was. I was then instructed to lead the Highland Brigade towards Burgersdorp – with two thousand men and guns to pull, a good twenty-four-hour journey. Gorringe would meanwhile do his best to find a fourth regiment – essential to my proposed entrapment of the Boer army.

Sneaking up on the Boer is well-nigh impossible, especially when travelling with a large contingent of men and wagons. But, somehow, we managed to get into position without their fleeing. We had them surrounded, apart from the final pass, and had been informed that the vital battalion would be in position there by the morning. There was a tremendous sense of excitement and anticipation amongst us all. The Boer appeared unsettled; they clearly knew we were there.

In the pitch black that night I lay motionless on the same hill as before, looking down on their camp. The fires were still burning and we could hear noise from below. My heart was hammering and I was incredibly anxious; having come up with the assault plan, I was desperate for it to succeed. But at first light, when I looked down, to my shock and consternation, there wasn't a single person remaining. They had slipped out through the fourth pass.

There was enormous disappointment throughout the brigade, and I had never felt so tired or so miserable. After four nights with little sleep and a hundred and twenty miles on horseback, we'd missed out on a sitting target. It was the lowest point of my army career.

Our next project was to provide cover for the engineers who were building a row of blockhouses to control the movement of people and to stop the railway tracks from being blown. It was a tedious job, but at least we wouldn't have to man the buildings afterwards. They were erected five hundred yards apart with stone walls at the base, wood and corrugated iron above, and they housed a dozen men apiece. Barbed wire was strung between each one and rockets were set up to fire if the wire was cut and went slack, should the Boer try to get themselves and horses through.

There was a large Boer Commando unit of two hundred men that had been causing trouble in our district, and so we formed a plan to drive them towards the line of blockhouses, by then manned by the Connaught Rangers. It was exactly like a grouse shooting, with a hundred of us Scouts and two hundred or so from other units lined up along ten miles. The officers kept the line straight, passing messages down the line using semaphore flags. But yet again, the Boer slipped away.

Chapter 18

Donald John, South Africa, 1901

It was midday. We had stopped to get some shade beneath gum trees and to eat a biscuit or two and drink some water. Captain MacDonald called the NCOs together and briefed them. The men were restless; they could tell there was a plan afoot.

After a quarter of an hour Cammy called everyone to form up, so that the adjutant could give orders. 'Men,' he began, 'as you know, General Kitchener has decided that the best way to bring the Boer farmers to heel is to burn their farms and crops and to take their families to camps. We have been spared this duty so far, but we have instructions to clear the land south of Edenburg and to escort the people to Aliwal North. We will do this with the best traditions of Highlanders in mind: firmly but with courtesy throughout.'

He went on to explain the mission in detail, outlining who was to do what and when. The men then split into groups and a great deal of grumbling could be heard. At one point I heard Cammy's voice rising above the others saying, 'You'll just do what you are told, Mackenzie!'

'Captain MacDonald,' I said, 'the men are very uncomfortable about burning the farms and herding the people away. Is there no way we can avoid it?'

'I understand,' he replied. 'I feel the same. But orders are orders, and if we don't do it, there will be hell to pay. Another regiment will take our place and they won't have the sympathy and kindness that our men have.'

I could see he was ill at ease and shared our concerns, but I felt compelled to go on. 'But, Captain, we've all heard what happened at Bethulie Bridge. We could be taking these innocent civilians to their death – surely that can't be right?' As I spoke I was aware that my voice was rising and my face was bright red. I was not one to display insubordination.

Captain MacDonald's furious retort took me by surprise. 'Gillies, get a grip of yourself!' he bellowed. 'You are in the army, you are a professional soldier, and you are subject to army discipline. One more word and I'll have you placed under arrest.'

After this reprimand I sat apart from the others, brooding over the exchange. Why hadn't there been a mutiny in the army over these clearances before now? Had people lost their sense of honour and decency? The very thought of having to visit a camp made me feel sick. I knew I wouldn't be able to help but look at the women and children there and see the faces of our own beloved. The old hands said we'd get used to it, but I for one knew I wouldn't. The refugee camps were constructed like military camps, with rows of tents, toilet blocks, a cooking area and so on. I did not doubt that the inhabitants hated us; they were resentful and distraught about their circumstances. I had even heard rumours that a great many of the babies and young children died there, the women, too, due to the poor hygiene. Disease was rife, so bad in fact that our men were forbidden from entering the camp, not that they wanted to.

It was in June 1901 that we were finally ordered to clear the farmland south of Edenburg. We knew by then that Lord Lovat had raised a second contingent of Scouts and we were due to head back to Scotland in a month or so. By this time our numbers had halved; there remained only about fifty of us.

Up until then, we had managed to avoid clearing land. Our CO, Colonel Murray, had apparently said to the generals that the Scouts hailed from areas where they themselves had been driven off their land, their houses burned and people herded onto ships bound for Nova Scotia and Australia. They knew the misery of it. Murray wasn't sure the Scouts would be prepared to do it, and in any case weren't we too valuable as a reconnaissance force?

However, our turn had come and there was nothing we could do about it. The plan was to move onto a *kopje* and spy the farm at dawn with a glass. There was a chance there would be men prepared to fight. After the job was done, we were to meet up with a convoy of wagons at Mafeteng and escort the families south.

It was a cold morning when we arrived at our rendezvous location. We could see smoke rising from a chimney, and the African workers leaving their shacks and heading off to tend to the cattle. A dog was barking in our direction; maybe it had caught our scent. Lieutenant Grant took a party of men a long way around the property, to come at it from the rear. We were tasked to approach from the front, at exactly noon.

As the morning progressed, we watched the Vanloos family coming and going. There was one man – a grey-bearded grandfather, probably too old to go off to fight – and four women and seven children. We counted at least twenty black workers, too. Everyone was to come, along with all the cattle, sheep and horses.

As we drew near, we could see the workers scurrying back to their houses. But what we didn't expect was that the grandfather would decide to conduct a battle of his own and start firing from a window.

Captain MacDonald shouted, 'Charge!'

At once we were galloping in from about a hundred yards away, me at the front, bullets whistling as they passed. My horse was hit square in the chest, and as it fell I was catapulted over its head. I landed heavily, only a few yards in front of the farmhouse, and everything went into slow motion. I looked up, winded and unable to move, to see this crazed old man staring down the barrel of his rifle, straight at me. I'll never forget that image: his deeply lined face, the sweat on his brow, and through the tangled mass of his grey hair and beard, his glittering black eyes. Then, just as I saw his finger tighten on the trigger, one of the women knocked his rifle up and the shot flew over my head. The woman and I looked intensely at each other for a second. She had saved my life.

The sound of gunfire, although only feet away, now seemed distant. The house was almost within touching distance. I stretched out my hand towards my saviour, but she was gone.

By now, Grant's men were in the house. The old man had been shot as he defended his property to the last. Still dazed, I lay on the ground where I had fallen for what seemed like an eternity, shaking like a leaf.

The woman reappeared, framed in the farmhouse window, and called out in English, 'Are you all right?'

I nodded, mouthed, 'Yes, thank you,' and smiled weakly. She disappeared into the house.

One of our men rushed over to see how I was. He handed me a flask of water, which I gulped down and then poured over my head. I thanked him as he pulled me to my feet. 'I thought I was a goner there. The old man had me right in his sights from point-blank range.'

What should have been a relatively trouble-free evacuation had turned into mayhem. The incident was all over in a few minutes, but the women and children were screaming at us. Two women suddenly came at us with a pitchfork and a kitchen knife. Cammy and I easily overpowered them, and within moments, they were lying face down in the dust, hands tied behind their backs.

'Tell them to behave themselves and we'll untie them, Donald John,' Cammy called over to me.

Stumbling over my words, I made it clear, as kindly as I could under the circumstances, that we intended to treat them well, but I only received a torrent of abuse. These two women were proving hard to be kind to.

Meanwhile, we gave the others twenty minutes to gather their personal belongings before we set fire to the buildings. I thought the screeching of the old man's wife was never going to end until Cammy threatened to gag her unless she promised to be quiet. I was again the interpreter though no one needed any understanding of Afrikaans to realise the extent of her distress.

The farm workers were ordered to dig a grave, two planks were tied together to make a cross, and Captain MacDonald recited the Lord's Prayer as the old man was lowered in.

The old man's wife, her two daughters and six children were placed in an open farm wagon pulled by two oxen. The other, much younger woman – my saviour – and her daughter had a small Scotch cart that they pulled along, with the help of a servant. A dog trotted beside them, barking constantly. I noticed that there seemed to be no love lost between this young woman and the other three.

The farm workers and their womenfolk – some with infants strapped to their backs and youngsters running alongside – trailed along at the back with twenty or more cattle and two hundred sheep.

We were stretched out for a good half-mile. The Scouts had spies front and back, and the rest took turns to ride to and fro, trying to keep the stragglers moving. We were sitting ducks for a Boer attack.

I was without a horse now, but was happy to walk. After a while, I asked the servant pulling the cart alongside the young woman and her daughter to let me take his place. We walked in silence for what seemed like hours, the woman never meeting my eyes. Their dog was a blue merle rough collie, the same size as our Border collies but with startlingly pale blue eyes. The poor beast was emaciated. It seemed to belong to the child and was wary of me at the outset, growling and then backing off. I've always loved dogs, though, and have a way with them. After some coaxing, we soon made friends.

It was far more of a challenge to befriend the woman or even get her to say a single word. Withdrawn and sullen, she stared straight ahead as she shouldered her share of the cart's weight. I understood, of course. She was in shock, a prisoner, but I was desperate to thank her for her courage.

I went ahead of the cart and picked up a stick, throwing it clear of the wheels. The dog raced after it and returned, dropping it at my feet, imploring me with its eyes to repeat the game. The young girl and I smiled, and even her mother, finally, caught my eye. The dog and I continued the game for a few minutes, with the girl joining in.

I held out my hand to the girl and said in Afrikaans, 'My name is Donald John.'

She took it, after glancing at her mother for approval. 'My name is Anja,' she replied.

I bent down and shook the dog's paw, looking up questioningly towards Anja.

'She is called Hondjie. She is my dog,' she announced proudly.

Her mother shook my hand. 'Linde,' she said, her voice low and guarded.

As we walked along we began to talk. Linde had a bit of English – her grandmother was from Cape Town, she explained – so we managed to understand each other. Anja told me that Hondjie means 'puppy' in Afrikaans, that she had been given her as a present when she was a small child, and they had hardly left each other's side since. At night, Linde added, she would invariably find the two curled up beside each other.

I was a little gushing towards Linde at first. But I soon became acutely aware that the other women were giving her filthy looks, no doubt thinking she was fraternising with the enemy. One of the women shouted the word '*hoer*' and Linde recoiled as if she'd been slapped.

'Do they know how you knocked the old man's gun aside and saved my life?' I asked.

She stared at me, and in a low voice replied, 'No. They would kill me if they knew. Don't talk about it now, please.'

Hearing this, I declared loudly that there was a problem with the cart wheel, and stopped to check it, allowing the others to move ahead. Once they were about fifty yards ahead, I wondered if she might relax a little. Linde still didn't smile and was reluctant to speak at all, so most of the talking was left to me.

'You saved my life, Linde. I cannot thank you enough.' I looked at her, but she was staring straight ahead. 'He was looking straight down the barrel at me. He couldn't have missed,' I continued, smiling. I was eager to show my gratitude, wanted her to like me.

She stopped pulling the cart and looked me straight in the eye. 'If you are so grateful, then why are you marching us to a death camp? You call it a refugee camp, but you are condemning us to death. You do know that, yes?'

I was horrified by her words. Anja was holding her mother's hand, hiding behind her skirt and looking up at me, wide-eyed.

'I'm sorry, so sorry,' I whispered.

She stared at me for a few moments and then raised her hand in acknowledgement. 'I know it's not your fault,' she replied quietly.

Her voice had attracted attention and a couple of soldiers came back to see what was going on. I assured them that all was well, and we resumed our walk, but in weary silence. My mind was racing. I had of course heard the rumours about the camps but, naively, had hoped they were exaggerated. No wonder these women hated us. But what could I do to save these two? Since Linde had saved me, I felt that I now had a personal responsibility to do something in return.

At that moment I heard ferocious barking and yelping. Hondjie had run on ahead, scavenging for some food, and had disappeared from view. I dropped the shaft of the cart and sprinted off towards the noise. A pack of four wild dogs had set upon her, defending the remains of an ox she had sniffed out. She was writhing around trying to escape as they mauled her. I waded in with my boots and fists flying, and soon there were jaws snapping, the wild dogs twisting and turning everywhere. I managed to grab Hondjie by the scruff of her neck and drag her out of the melee. Thankfully Captain MacDonald was there within seconds and, leaning down from his horse, began whipping the animals away, firing a couple of shots from his pistol at them for good measure as they slunk off into the veld.

By this time Anja was beside me, crying out her dog's name and stroking Hondjie, who was whimpering. I quickly examined the animal and turned to Anja. 'Don't worry,' I reassured her. 'It's not too bad. We'll tidy her up and she'll be as right as rain.'

The men surrounded us, all talking of their experiences of dog fights and offering advice on what best to do. Cammy pushed through with the company medic and told the men to get back to their posts.

Ten minutes later, Hondjie's wounds had been treated with iodine from the medic's pack and her leg was bandaged. A soldier found a scrap of dried meat for Hondjie, who seemed to be recovering from her ordeal, and we laid her in the cart. The crisis was over.

As we set off again, there was a change of attitude from Linde. Rescuing the dog seemed to have broken the ice. Looking me in the eye, she placed her hand on my arm and said, 'Thank you. Without you, Hondjie would be dead.'

Her warm words delighted me though I refrained from saying aloud what I was thinking: that without me and my fellow soldiers, Hondjie would not have been in this situation at all. 'Think nothing of it,' I replied, smiling at her. I wanted to continue talking to her, to find out more about her but held back. There would be time enough for that.

Captain MacDonald called a halt shortly after that and we settled down for the night, the Vanloos family apart from the men. The next morning, we were up and on our way at dawn. I hurried over to the Scotch cart to help. Anja was still exhausted and her mother encouraged her to climb onto the cart to sleep for a bit longer.

'Are you all right?' I asked. 'Did they give you a tough time?'

'It was fine,' she said, but from her tone I knew it wasn't.

I chattered away about myself to help pass the time. I told her I farmed sheep and cattle, was a joiner by trade, and lived in the most beautiful village in the world, in the Highlands of Scotland, with a sandy beach which looked south over the sea to mountains beyond. Although I suspect she understood little of it, I couldn't help telling her the Ardnish parable, as told to me by my grandfather:

After Adam and Eve's time, God told all his people that they needed to come and meet Him on the Sabbath at noon and He would give them land where they could live with their spouses and rear children. But Donald Gillies was late and didn't arrive until well past the appointed hour. The Lord looked down on him and said, 'My child, you are late, why is that?'

Donald Gillies replied that he had been busy feeding the sheep and cows otherwise his people would go hungry.

The Lord saw that he was a good man and took pity on him, saying, 'Well, my son, I was keeping the best place on earth for myself. It's called Ardnish, and it is there you should live and not leave until I come down to earth once more.'

Chapter 19

Donald John, Ardnish, 1944

I can see the dawn breaking through the windows. Another
night has passed. The wind is increasing, a westerly; I can
tell by the sound it makes coming down the chimney. We
are well sheltered here, from all but the warmer southerly.
It wasn't so long since we moved from the old blackhouse
next door into the post office building. The thatch of our
old house was finished and cold draughts came whistling
through the gappy stone walls, but this place has a decent
slate roof and paving-stone floor.

The sleet is splattering against the glass now, and there's
a drip-drip-drip into the bucket from the leak none of us
somehow can find. The snow will return later, I feel sure. I
was a fisherman for a while, and we avoided going out on
days like this. The weather could change suddenly from
good to bad and we would find ourselves rowing for dear
life towards land.

As the wind picks up and howls down the chimney I
think of my dear old friend and neighbour, Ewan. Mairi's
late husband was on the herring boats. He would tell us
stories of storms that would scare you to death just hearing

about them. He was off the Flannan Isles one day, and the sky was as dark as night to the southwest, and they were on the wrong side of the island when the gale came. They could see the lighthouse flashing its warning light, much too close to them for comfort. The Flannan Isles have a terrible reputation amongst Hebridean folk for being 'the devil's islands'. One crew member was a lad, just fourteen, on his first voyage. Ewan knew the family, a widow with this only child.

He had warned the captain to keep well clear of the islands. There were plenty of fish there but for a good reason: the locals kept out of the area. But this man was from Peterhead and no one knew better than himself.

There were five men on board desperately pulling the nets in, tying down the anchor, spars and everything else that could move. The skipper had both sails up, cutting it fine, desperately trying to get north of the land. The hold had three tons of herring in it, so the boat was sitting low and heavy in the water.

It was late morning when the first gust caught the sails. The boat tilted forty-five degrees and Ewan could feel the fish slide to one side. The mast seemed certain to break.

'Haul them down!' the skipper shouted. As the gale caught the loose canvas it writhed and flapped, and the men fought to stop the sails blowing into the water. By now the boat was plunging up and down, the sea coming over the sides, tens of tons at a time. The lad was caught at the stern, picked up by the water, bounced against the hold covers and swept along the deck past Ewan as he clung to the railing. Ewan said later that the lad actually knocked against him, his eyes looking, terrified, into Ewan's from inches away, his hands fruitlessly trying to clutch at anything to prevent the inevitable. Ewan said that if he'd let go to help, he, too, would have been sent overboard. By this time, the boat was close to the cliffs, and the roar of the surf against the rocks was deafening, the spray shooting fifty feet into the air. It seemed they had only a slim chance of getting past. Even the non-believers on the boat were praying for salvation.

They could see the three lighthouse men, dressed in their yellow oilskins and sou'westers, standing on the rocks only yards away ready to help – so close that Ewan could make out their frantic expressions. Somehow the boat made it past the rocks, but there was no let-up for the rest of the day and all through the night. Two men were working the pumps an hour at a time, and every now and again someone would go down to check the water level in the bilges. One of the hatch covers blew off and Ewan rushed forward, in the dark, with a piece of canvas and rope to cover the hole. He told us that balancing with his feet against the handrail, a loose rope lashing his face and every couple of minutes a wall of water trying to rip him from his position, was the most terrifying moment of his life. The old boat was creaking and groaning as it was pummelled by the elements, and they all knew that if a plank went, it would be the end of them.

At last the storm abated. The crew slumped where they were, shocked and exhausted, unable to move or speak, each one contemplating with dread telling the boy's mother of his death when they returned to Mallaig.

Ewan himself was swept off a deck a year or two later, leaving Mairi as yet another fisherman's widow and their baby boy Sandy alone at Peanmeanach with us. He'd told me that he would die at sea, but all the same he was far too young to go. Fishing was the most perilous of work, even if the money was good. I'd always been happier with my feet on the ground and in my own bed every night.

While we were in South Africa, a great mystery happened on the Flannan Isles. One of the Hebridean lads, a minister's son, received a letter from his father and read it aloud to us. Everyone was transfixed, and it was discussed for days. It told of a night in December 1900 when a relief lighthouse keeper was being taken out to the island. When they anchored up, he went ashore. There was no sign of the three men there on duty, only uneaten food and an upside-down chair. Two oilskin coats were gone, but not the third, and entries in the log revealed the terror they endured during a great storm that had raged for three days. But the authorities on the neighbouring island of Lewis disputed the account, saying there had been no storm at all then; the sea had been calm. The bodies were never washed up, which was very rare and in itself needed explaining. 'The Devil has claimed three souls,' the minister wrote.

Mairi will be up along the row. She's always been the first to rise in the village. On a still day I can hear her loom through the wall as the shuttle clanks back and forth. Today she might wait a bit, seeing she has Father Angus staying. Demand for her tweed is good; she can sell as much as she can make. All of the clothing factories are busy making military uniforms so a brightly coloured tweed is a popular gift for rich women to give to their menfolk when they're on leave.

It was a wild day like this that Ewan came to grief. He was from St Kilda and they knew all about bad weather out there. He used to tell me of the islands – Hirta, Boreray and Stac an Armin, with its six hundred-foot-high stack – and the gannets, petrels and puffins so thick in the air above the sea cliffs you couldn't see the sky. Eighty-five people lived there when he left as a boy. He would have been terribly sad to know that the last few people, facing starvation and sickness, had asked to be evacuated fourteen years ago.

Ewan was delivering a very old fishing boat to a man on Soay but never arrived. He set off from Oban and was coming around Ardnamurchan Point when he must have been washed off the deck. The lighthouse man at Ardnamurchan had noted that the boat was heading north under sail with gale force winds coming from the west. His body was found at Ardtoe and the boat itself smashed to pieces on the west end of Eilean Shona. The forecast had been for fine weather, but the storm had come out of nowhere. The man who was due to help him had dropped out so Ewan had foolishly decided to set sail alone.

I'd love to have visited St Kilda. I remember Ewan's son Sandy talking about going out to see a cousin who still lived there at the time. He and Donald Peter were just lads, and they had a plan to get the MacBrayne ferry across to Harris and then get a ride out on a fishing boat. They planned to stay a few weeks, living on fish and mutton – he told me there were sheep on the island – but somehow it never came to pass. I've seen photographs of Village Bay, with its curved inlet, the remains of a volcano and the twenty houses in a semi-circle following the curve of the pebbled beach. The manse and Protestant church sat on the right, and the hillside was crisscrossed in a lattice of small fields with cleits, wee stone huts that were used to store the feathers and oil from the fulmars they harvested.

The door opens and Angus asks how my night was, if I managed to sleep a bit.

'Och, not really, but it was fine,' I reassure him. 'I have my memories. I enjoy leafing through them in the small hours.'

'He was coughing and spluttering all night and his chest is full of phlegm he can't clear,' Louise pipes up. 'I think we should get the doctor again. I could go now.'

I shake my head. 'No, don't you worry. He couldn't do anything when he came last time, and anyway, it's a priest I'm needing, not a doctor.'

Chapter 20

Donald John, South Africa, 1901

The next day we found ourselves right at the front of the convoy. There was a problem with a wagon and an order was given for us to stop and wait. Stretched behind us were men off their horses, giving them a rest. Tired, too, the three of us lay on a bank in silence. I looked across at Linde. Her eyes were shut, her arm draped over Anja who was curled up asleep.

Linde was beautiful; there was no doubt of that. Golden skin, freckles, a mouth that turned up at the edges. Her fair hair was tied back, apart from a wisp that lay across her face. I felt an urge to reach across and tuck it behind her ear. Boer women invariably wore large, wide-rimmed bonnets to keep the sun off their heads, but Linde was an exception.

I looked away, suddenly blushing. I'd been staring at her. Thank goodness she hadn't seen me. And thank goodness she was no longer hostile to me. I had the dog to thank for that.

Hondjie was lying on her back, tail wagging as I scratched her tummy. The dog was greatly loved by Anja and her mother, and they enjoyed watching me playing with her or regaling them with one of my dog stories.

'That dog likes you,' said Linde, her eyes open now.

'She'd like anyone who tickled her tummy,' I replied with a smile. 'We have a collie for working the sheep at home. In fact we're never without a dog or two on the farm. Our neighbour, Johnny Bochan, has seventeen.' I found myself using the word 'farm' to impress her, when what I really meant was 'croft', just a few barren acres.

The farm workers were nearby, tending to a few goats.

'There is a wee island just off the beach, where my grandfather would keep his billy goat, although he called the males "bucks". On Goat Island, about a mile away, there were half a dozen females, so in the autumn there would be a day when the men would capture the buck, load him into the boat and take him off for his annual visit. Getting him there was easy – he knew what was going on! – but trying to catch him a month later and bring him back was another thing altogether.'

We both laughed at this, me blushing once more.

I tried to think of another story which would steer us back into less awkward territory. I told her about an old English colonel who was a great friend of Christian Cameron-Head at Inverailort. The two men had met in their youth in London and remained great friends. Every October for many years he would come up to stay for a week and shoot a stag or two during the rut. As a result, he got to know the stalkers well. The colonel was a lifelong confirmed bachelor, and after he died he was one of the first people to be cremated in Glasgow. His ashes were sent back up to the castle and a case of whisky was left in his will to the two stalkers, with the instruction that his ashes should be scattered on Loch Ailort. So they rowed to the middle of the loch, with one stalker on the oars and the other carefully holding the urn. They agreed on a spot, whereupon the tin box was tossed overboard. But the wind caught it and it floated determinedly towards the north shore. The stalkers were alarmed. 'He'll land at Polnish!' one of them exclaimed. 'Oh, no, he won't,' said the other and, picking up his rifle, he fired a couple of shots into the urn and it sank.

'Why did you join the army?' Linde asked.

'Money and adventure, really. It's what men in the Highlands of Scotland have done for generations. Our general says we're the backbone of the British Army.'

I told Linde how the Highlanders were known to be great soldiers, bragging that, with the skirl of the pipes, kilts blowing in the wind and bayonets fixed, even the bravest enemy would turn and run. Because of the hard conditions in the Highlands, for decades men had taken the King's shilling and signed up. I told her about the Massacre of Glencoe when the Campbells were guests of the Macdonalds and were ordered to rise up in the middle of the night and put their hosts to the sword. Then I told her about 1715 and Bonnie Prince Charlie and the rising at Glenfinnan in 1745, and the subsequent disaster at Culloden. By the end of the day she was fairly steeped in my history, asking endless questions and regaling Anja with simplified versions of the dramatic parts.

After all my tales of battle she wanted to know if all the men were rough in Scotland, fighting all the time, or were others kind, like me. I fancied she had a twinkle in her eye when she said this. I also felt that this was the first time she fully relaxed and warmed to me.

I explained to her that Highlanders were gentle people really; it was the incomers who were rough. The building of the railway to Mallaig had brought some bad sorts to the area who would drink and fight amongst themselves. There were police in nearby Arisaig and Glenfinnan now, whereas before, the nearest had been in Fort William, thirty miles away.

'Glencoe, Culloden – it seems you always lose,' she said, teasing me. 'Will you lose the war against the Boer, too?'

I hesitated, squirming uncomfortably. 'There are ten British soldiers for every one Boer fighter. I'm sure we won't lose this time,' I said quietly. 'But enough of all my stories. I must be boring you with them. It's your turn now.'

'No, tell us more,' she insisted. 'But speak a little slower, please, and use simpler words. Sometimes I find it difficult to keep up.'

As we progressed, a herd of gazelles came close to the convoy. A couple of the Scouts, determined to improve our rations, shot at them, and managed to hit one. It dropped to the ground and was brought back to great acclaim.

'There aren't gazelles in Scotland, are there?' asked Linde hesitantly.

'No, we have red deer. They're about three times the size of a gazelle; the meat of one would feed our village for a whole week.'

I told her that when I was growing up, when someone local had a fight, it always involved deer. When the Camerons at Inverailort Castle appointed a new game-keeper – young and single, called Calum Sinclair, he hailed from the north – he was overly keen to establish his author-ity. The three sons of Lottie MacDonald of Laggan were accustomed to rowing across to Alisary and helping themselves to a hind or stag from the corrie between An Stac and Roshven hill.

Sinclair took exception to this and tried to drive them off, threatening to call the police. The MacDonald boys were furious, arguing that they'd taken deer off the hill for generations and weren't about to stop now. They gave Sinclair a bit of a hiding and tied him up in his cottage. The next day, feeling guilty, they went back over with a dram and some food for him, and before long they all became fast friends, even coming to an arrangement about an occasional deer for the pot.

I told her that Lottie MacDonald himself had shot a stag at Alisary, and as he came to gralloch it, realised that he'd forgotten his *sgian-dubh*. He had two options. He could either try to get the carcass to the boat intact, which would be far too heavy, or he could go home and get a knife which, with the boat trip across the loch, would take half a day. He came up with a third option which was to rip open the animal's chest with his teeth and thereafter pull out the stomach.

I enjoyed the astonishment on Linde's face at the end of that story!

Anja had been quiet and serious at the outset of our journey, but it seemed that she and I had become firm friends over the past few days. She was ten years old, such a sweet girl with curly, flaxen hair and a pretty embroidered dress. I think she could see how much I enjoyed her mother's company and how helpful I was with the cart. I gave her a chunk of chocolate which I had in my bag and she loved it – she'd never tasted it before.

'You are kind to my daughter,' said Linde. 'She likes you.'

'And I like her, too. She's a lovely lass.' Then, tentatively, I added, 'Where is her father?'

'I don't want to talk about that,' she replied firmly.

I knew she meant it, and we walked on in silence for some time until, suddenly, Linde began speaking, her voice cracking. 'Sometimes I forget you are taking us to a concentration camp and . . .' She began to sob quietly.

I reached out to console her, but she pushed me away and clutched Anja close to her.

I always tried to be discreet when I was around Linde, but the other men had begun to tease me about being so attached to her, and soon Captain MacDonald took me aside. 'Everyone is aware of how much time you spend with that young woman,' he said firmly, his voice laden with disapproval. 'I'm going to get one of the others to lend you his horse, and you can go ahead with the advance party.'

It wasn't phrased as an order, but it was one. Of course, he was thinking of my Morag back at home, and trying to protect me from temptation. But I was stung, and remonstrated strongly. 'Yes, sir. But if I may, tomorrow I'd like to help her again. Her own family are all dead and she's hated by her in-laws. I believe she sees me as her protector.' I felt the weakness of my entreaty as I uttered the words. I could tell he wasn't persuaded. I tried again, telling him how she had knocked the old Boer's rifle out of the way and saved my life. But her actions didn't justify what he saw as my amorous intentions towards the woman. We left it like that, but I knew I wouldn't stop gravitating towards her.

'Sir, I can't stop thinking about the camp at Aliwal North. The women believe they are being taken there to die.'

MacDonald said nothing in response, so I continued: 'Even though we are soldiers with our orders, should we, as Christians, take civilians to their death?' I looked at him anxiously. Would he bellow at me again, or respond as an old friend?

'Donald John, I know how much this worries you, and if I thought we were taking these people to a death camp then I wouldn't do it. You've heard of Emily Hobhouse, haven't you? She's becoming involved and is already improving the conditions within the camps. Linde doesn't know the truth about what is happening.'

'But she fears the worst, sir,' I said. 'She's terrified for her daughter.'

He sighed. 'I don't believe it's quite so bad as she imagines. You know what happens to rumours once they start to spread. They get worse and worse. I truly think that Mrs Hobhouse has the situation under control.'

I knew that in December, the humanitarian Emily Hobhouse had come across from England to inspect the camps. She was horrified by the deprivation she witnessed and coined the term 'concentration camps'. Once back in Britain, she submitted a report to the British Government and launched a campaign that was causing a stir.

I was reassured by his statement and left with a lighter step.

Chapter 21

Donald John, Ardnish, 1944

I'm wide awake now, alert and enjoying the reminiscing. I cast my mind back, flit through the highlights of my life: from winning the hand of my wife and the birth of our children to being singled out for my carpentry skills by Professor Blackburn on the completion of Roshven House ... My pride in Angus becoming a priest and my grandson winning the Highland Society medal at the Northern Meeting Piping competition ... All of them good times, to be sure.

Of course I think of the difficult times, too: the shock of losing my leg, Linde and Anja, my son dying in the prime of his life, and my family coming close to starvation before I set off to fight in the Boer War. But I shake off these dark thoughts.

By God, we've had some fun here. I smile to myself as the images crowd in. In my youth our festivities took place at New Year – Hogmanay being a much bigger celebration in the Highlands than Christmas. The villagers took turns to host the Hogmanay ceilidh. When I was a boy there were over two hundred people on Ardnish, so there were

often as many as seventy or eighty in Peanmeanach on the
night. There was a fiddler and a box player, plus my father
and myself with the pipes. Father had me practising the
chosen tunes for days beforehand. The young kicked things
off with a couple of dances – usually the Eightsome Reel or
the Schottische – and then the adults joined in. Everyone
did a 'turn' – a poem, song or story – and not a word of
English was spoken; few spoke anything but Gaelic back
then. The tables were laden with fruitcake, scones and
oatcakes. And of course there was plenty of whisky, not a
drop of it legal, and gallons of beer. No matter how poor
we were at the time, there was always a good meal to be
had at Hogmanay.

On the stroke of midnight there was a call for hush, and
then came a rap on the door. '*Failte!*' the host cried as he
threw it open – welcome! – and in strode a tall, dark, handsome stranger bearing a tray with coal, salt and a dram of
whisky. Everyone then made their way around the gathering, kissing and shaking hands, exchanging best wishes for
the year ahead, and the songs and chatter went on all night.
Invariably someone disgraced himself – a young lad getting
sick, a couple caught having a cuddle out the back, or,
more usually, a man falling over dead drunk while his wife
scolded him.

That was just the start of it. With heads already pounding, we headed off first-footing to all the clachans of Sloch,
Laggan, Mullochbuie and Polnish. My parents carried two
bottles of whisky with them. We started from the house
around mid-morning on the first of January and didn't get
back for a couple of days, until we'd been by everyone,
toasted in the New Year and wished each other good health

and happiness for the year ahead. It was quite a ritual, and it meant everyone got to know each other well; a lot of good came out of it as the elderly and the sick all received a visit.

The only person who didn't welcome first-footers, I remember, was Margaret Macleod, the fierce school teacher at Polnish. She was an ardent member of the Free Church from Harris, who didn't drink and loudly damned us all to hell for celebrating a pagan ritual like Hogmanay.

I wake with a start to the sound of Angus's voice asking if I'm all right. I must have dozed off, muttering to myself.

The snow has stopped and the wind has blown itself out. It appears Angus has been in and out, carrying peat and doing other heavy jobs to help the women.

'The snow is about eight inches deep, Father,' he reports, 'but I'll warrant it'll be a foot deeper in places where it's drifted. Louise was relieved that the sheep were sheltered last night.'

'What about the cow?' I ask.

'She's fine, too. Mairi's milking her right now. She'll be calving in a couple of months.'

I cross myself, as has been my habit all my life, and both Angus and I laugh. The annual birth of a calf is so vital to a crofting family. I suspect I must have seen an old woman do it in my youth.

'When do you need to get back to the 51st Division, Angus?' I see him hesitate.

'Och, there's no hurry. They've got another priest there at the moment. I was due to be at the cathedral for a while, but we've plenty of priests and the Archbishop said I should stay here as long as I want. We normally have a few away doing missionary work, but the war has stopped all that, so they're not short-staffed.'

'Do you keep in touch with those you met at the seminary?' I ask.

'Well, they came from all over. Us Gaelic speakers from Lochaber and the islands are mostly in the Oban diocese and don't pass through Edinburgh much. But Archbishop Andrew, being a Lochaber man himself, always keeps a special eye out for those of us from the west.'

Angus works directly for the Archbishop, who is the brother of my good friend Colonel Willie. He has visited Peanmeanach several times, and on those occasions we often headed to the loch for some trout fishing and a blether. I think of the colonel too. We made a good team in the Boer War, and when I came back after having my leg amputated, he not only made sure I got my army pension, but he also had a special saddle made for me that allowed me to balance better on the pony.

He died in 1939, only a couple of months after war had been declared. When you are old, little beats a good funeral, and his, held on St Andrew's Day at St Margaret's, Roybridge, was one of the best. Donald Angus, Morag and I attended. My son Angus himself was the celebrant, assisting the Archbishop in commemorating his brother, with a good three hundred and fifty in attendance. I remember thinking I was the oldest person there.

A party of eight Lovat Scouts, including my grandson, came down from Beauly for the funeral. My heart swells with pride at the memory. Two handsome, glossy black horses pulled the hearse from the village, and Morag and myself followed in a charabanc, kindly arranged by the colonel's son, Andrew. Once all the mourners had found lifts in a variety of trucks and cars, or on horseback, or had marched the three miles from the church, everyone got ready to climb up the hill to the beautiful graveyard. Mary MacInnes, a famed beauty who lived at the bottom of the hill at Cille Choirill, passed tea around as everyone gathered.

Uniformed Lovat Scouts formed the main bearer party and alongside them were the farm and distillery workers. At the foot of the Cille Choirill brae, Lord Lovat, looking immaculate, gave the order: 'Pick up the coffin.' Halfway up, the second order was given: 'Put down the coffin.' There, Andrew 'drammed' the coffin bearers, no doubt with Long John's best whisky, served in a vast silver quaich, before the coffin was again hoisted shoulder high.

Donald Angus played the lament, the mournful 'Flowers Of The Forest', as my oldest friend was lowered into the dark Lochaber soil. I struggled to hold back my tears.

Chapter 22

Donald John, South Africa, 1901

Linde, Anja and I found that we had once again drifted
apart from the rest of the convoy. Occasionally a soldier
would ride back to see how we were getting on, as even the
slowest wagon was way ahead, but most of the time it was
just we three and Hondjie. She had made a remarkable
recovery from her injuries and was no longer even
limping.

I was impressed by their stamina. We covered miles
every day with few complaints, and I often found myself
watching Linde: her determined stride, the way her
blonde hair shone under the sun's rays, and the moist
sheen of perspiration on her forehead. At one point, she
stopped to laugh freely at the antics of Anja and the dog,
and threw back her head. I felt my heart lurch at the
beauty of her.

Later that morning, a soldier rode up to me and produced
a letter from his saddlebag. It was from Morag. I turned it
over in my hands.

'Your wife?' Linde asked, raising an eyebrow.

I nodded.

'Then you must stop and read it.'

I hesitated. A cold feeling of discomfort filled my body. Shaking my head, I stuffed the letter in my pocket and resumed our trek.

That evening, after we had made camp by a stream, I finally opened the letter.

My dear husband,

You are on the other side of the world, leading a different life from us here. You have sunshine and long days. Our winter is dragging slowly by. We have wind and rain, and are in bed by six in the dark with no kerosene.

Life is hard here without you. With Angus away at Roshven working on the estate for two weeks and Sheena courting in Glenuig, it is just Donald Peter and me.

We badly need money. Can you arrange for some to get to us? Food is becoming scarce. We haven't had sugar or tea for over a month and mutton and kale keeps us alive but barely nourished . . .

I read on: neighbours were leaving Ardnish for Melbourne and Antigonish in Nova Scotia; there were not enough strong people in the village to launch a boat to fish; and the Fergusons' cow had given birth to a dead calf. I was overcome with guilt at being absent while Morag and the family suffered so much.

As I returned the letter to its envelope with a heavy heart, Linde joined me. 'Do you want to talk, Donald John?'

I nodded though I was uncertain whether I really did want to talk or not. I gazed into the distance, trying to formulate my thoughts.

Linde persevered. 'Is everything all right back home? Why don't you tell me about it?'

'Maybe it would be best if I drew it,' I replied. I took out a notepad and pencil from my bag in the wagon, and settled down to draw. Anja leant on my shoulder, watching carefully. As I drew, I talked.

I told them that the walls of Ardnish homes are built from stone dug up from the field or taken from the riverbed. The corners are rounded, not at ninety degrees. Two glazed windows at the front and a door in the middle. The roof is turf, covered in reeds that we gather every two or three years from the banks of the loch in the middle of the peninsula, and finally we throw an old fishing net over it all and tie rocks along the edges to keep the thatch from blowing off during a winter's gale.

'It looks lovely, so small and neat.' Linde smiled, examining my sketch. 'And where is the sea? Where are the mountains? Draw the village.'

I did a rough sketch of Peanmeanach and the surrounding area, pointing out the singing sands beach where we swim on hot summer days, the moss where the peat is cut, and the big house at Roshven where I'd worked on and off for the last twenty years.

I realised I had made it all sound idyllic and ridiculously romantic, and felt a pang of guilt. 'Actually, Linde, the Vanloos farm was much nicer than ours,' I confessed after a pause, and I decided to tell her the truth. That the dwellings were called blackhouses due to the smoke from the fire inside; that the floor was bare earth; that there was no running water and we had to walk to the burn to fill the kettle. That the children didn't wear shoes except on the worst of winter days when they would wear their parents' old boots to school and they each had to take a piece of peat or a lump of coal for the school fire.

But at the same time, I was desperate for her not to think of us as impoverished peasants and so I went to great lengths to explain how sophisticated and well educated our people were and how they thrived all over the world. I didn't want Linde to pity me, so I moved onto safer ground and started talking about the livestock at home. I knew Anja loved animals and I spoke as slowly as I could to make sure she understood.

I told Anja about our sheep, that in the Highlands we had indisputably the most handsome sheep in the whole world, that they were quite small and had black faces, and had the most beautiful lambs. I described how Morag reared newborn lambs in a box beside the fire in the kitchen. The same old whisky bottle would be filled with cow's milk and the children would squabble over who would feed them. After a couple of weeks, the lambs became noisy and naughty and would prance around the kitchen with their tails twitching madly. Morag would shoo them out to be with the other sheep when they were old enough, but from then on, they would always come up and butt your leg with their heads, demanding food or a scratch behind the ear. I told Anja, in my most serious voice, that tame sheep were a menace.

I admitted that we were much poorer at home than the farmers here, that finding any food in late winter was a real

worry and that many children died young. Linde was sceptical, pointing out how smart the Scouts looked in their
uniforms and their fine horses. I said we only had one cow
and some sheep, and that we would make some money
from helping the laird when he needed a wall built, or had
gentlemen staying who wanted to be taken deer stalking.
We survived on potatoes, oats and herring from the sea,
and were lucky to live by the shore as we had fish to eat
and seaweed to fertilise the land. It was much tougher to
eke out an existence in the remote glens.

Linde asked why my fingers often twitched so rhythmi-
cally, and I explained that it was the habit of many pipers
as we had hundreds of tunes in our heads. I talked about
the bagpipes and how my home of Ardnish was famous for
its piping; after all, we had the legendary Donald
MacDonald, himself a Scout, the MacDougalls from Sloch
and our own family, the hereditary pipers for the Lords of
the Isles.

'The pipes are played for pleasure,' I said, 'at weddings,
at parties, at funerals. When I play, everyone stops what
they're doing and listens, tapping their feet in time with the
tune.'

Linde had never heard them played, and when I mimed
a rendition of a march, then a jig, we were soon convulsing
with laughter. My pipes were at the military camp at Aliwal
North and I promised to play them for her as soon as I
could.

I could see in the distance that Captain MacDonald had
gathered the officers around him, and Cammy was there,
too. The rest of us would be called in for a briefing shortly.

'What is your wife like, may I ask? Linde said quietly.

I looked away. I did not want to have this conversation.

'Well . . .' I faltered, 'Morag is the hardest worker you ever met, the person who makes things happen in the village. She's a tremendous mother, maybe the best shepherd – male or female – in the Highlands, and she loves plants and animals—'

'And,' Linde cut in, 'is she a good wife?'

I squirmed at her frankness. 'We've been married for over twenty years, and while we have our differences we are doing just fine . . .' I could tell she wanted to know more. 'Put it this way, I was keen to come out here for a while.'

I knew Linde could sense that this was as much as I was prepared to tell her. I already felt as though I'd betrayed Morag by not praising her highly enough, and alluding to our difficulties. 'This is a little unfair. You know everything about my home and my life, so won't you tell me something about yourself?'

Linde looked away. 'I'm not sure you are in a position to tell me what is fair and what is not,' she said softly. 'I am your prisoner.'

I was chastened. 'Oh, Linde, I'm sorry . . .'

'It's all right.' She smiled a little. 'I think I pushed you to reveal something about your life, you did not want to, so I will tell you my story.'

She checked on Anja, who was fast asleep in the cart, and shifted closer towards me. We were almost touching.

'It is not a happy story,' she began matter-of-factly.

'I have no wish to upset you or force you to tell me things about yourself,' I said.

'I know that.' She looked straight into my eyes and my heart skipped a beat. 'I arrived from Heilbron, a hundred and fifty miles west of Bloemfontein, thirteen years ago. I worked for a farmer's wife as a mother's help, and there I met their neighbour, Johan Vanloos. We were married for eleven years and he was killed . . . six months ago . . . before you and your soldiers arrived.'

'I am sorry,' I whispered.

'Don't be.' I thought I could detect a harder edge to her voice. 'Johan's mother bossed me about. I was never good enough for her son. My place was to be in the house, to have his food ready, to make clothes, not to be heard. I was there to bear his children. She blamed me for not having more children, a son in particular. She said I was too precious to work hard. And as for Johan, well, he was never happy with anything. My cooking, my housework, how I dressed. I don't think I ever loved him, really, but I was resigned to spending the rest of my life with him.'

'For better or for worse,' I said.

She nodded. 'It could have been worse, though. He worked outside all day, every day, and he went to bed as early as he could. On Sundays we spent the whole day at the Reform Church. Anja is the best thing that came from him.'

Linde glanced nervously at her daughter. She was sound asleep.

'In the year before he died, he started drinking heavily. I don't know why. I came to dread his footsteps in the night, the stumbling around and the cursing. He forced himself on me . . . It was awful . . . Then he would just roll over and fall asleep, snoring. I would lie there wide awake, lonely . . . violated.'

I shook my head.

'He would get up in the morning without a word, still in the same filthy clothes, and leave me there. Never a hint of apology.'

I did not know what to say. I could barely look at her.

'After Johan died,' she went on after a pause, 'his brother took over the farm. He provided for Anja and me, but it was very clear that I was not wanted there. They started dropping hints about how I might be better off moving away. You know, Donald John, in my darkest hours, I was terrified they might try to get rid of me and keep Anja. My daughter is my life. She is everything. Everything else is gone: all that remains is the two of us.'

A long silence followed Linde's words. We trudged on in the heat. No one was behind us; there were only a few soldiers talking among themselves ahead of us and a heavy screen of dust between them and us.

There was a question I was burning to ask. I thought I knew the answer, but needed to hear it from Linde. 'How did Johan die?'

She was looking straight ahead and, try as I might, I couldn't read her feelings. 'He was on commando,' she replied eventually. 'They were attacking a convoy and he was shot – that's all I know. Everyone else at the farm found out before me. My mother-in-law knew two days before she told me. She thought I wouldn't care.

'I have been reluctant to tell you that my own father also fought in the war against the British. I just think you need to know.'

I nodded, unsurprised, but was touched that she wanted to tell me.

'He was a wonderful father to me, kind and caring. I can barely remember my mother; she died when I was a small child. Later, my father brought up my brother's son all alone. I was proud of him.'

'And when did he pass on?'

'He was killed last year, too. He hadn't wanted to fight. He loved my mother but she was long gone, and he adored the farm, and couldn't see why the war was necessary. He was too old, really, but he was forced to join up by his neighbours so he planned to do his bit as quickly as possible and then head home.'

'What happened?'

'He and my brother's son were in the Heilbron Commando, at a place called Spioenkop. They were hold-ing a hill to stop the British using it to shell our men.'

'My God, Spioenkop! Everyone has heard of that place. It was a disaster – well, it was a disaster for the British anyhow.'

'It may seem odd to you, but father and grandson had the same name: Wynand Sarel Roelofse.'

'Oh, I'm used to families where everyone has the same name. There's always a Donald Gillies in our family. I'm known throughout Ardnish as Donald Auch. Auch means "field" in Gaelic, because we have the big field behind our house. There's a Donald Gillies in Morar called Donald the Fish, because he's a well-known salmon poacher.'

She smiled. 'My brother was a Wynand, too, but he died many years ago, along with his wife. They tipped over in their wagon going across the Waterval River and drowned. That's why my nephew was bought up by my father. He was known as "Old W.S.". My cousin Christiaan was at

Spioenkop with them. I have heard the story of the battle many times from him. Do you know it?'

'A little, but tell me about it if you like. As long as it does not upset you too much.'

'It is good to talk about it all. It helps me to remember them. It was January. The British were under siege at Ladysmith, and your army had come to break the siege. Christiaan's people had been watching the British gathering down by the river and knew that an attack would come; they had seen guns being dragged up Mount Alice across the valley. General Botha was supposed to be on his way with reinforcements, but Christiaan's men had good positions, with stone walls in front. They'd been waiting a whole week, watching a distant fight on the black mountains. There were only about ninety men, all expecting an attack.

'My father was seventy-two then, his grandson only fourteen. The two of them had begged to join the same Commando unit together. They were incredibly close because they had been together for a long time, just the two of them. Anyway, there they were at night, asleep behind the wall, in the rain and the dark. They were caught unawares by the British soldiers. Christiaan saw Young WS leap up, grab his grandfather's arm and run off the hill, only just ahead of the enemy.

'General Botha was arriving at the base of the *kopje* by then, bringing men he had gathered together in the dawn. They were able to climb up the hill in such a way that those on the top couldn't see over the edge, and, suddenly, they were on the summit. Bullets were flying everywhere!

'WS and the others knew the enemy were close. They could see shells exploding just over the ridge and could hear the British soldiers screaming. My father and the others quickly gathered rocks and built defences out of sight of the British.

'Old WS was a fantastic rifle shot. Christiaan told me he had positioned himself off to the side, behind an acacia bush, with his grandson alongside him. Then the British suddenly came into view, and Christiaan's men felt very exposed. But the English men were silhouetted against the morning sun.

'WS killed many British, Donald John. He was firing as quickly as he could reload and he had the best vantage point.'

I did my best to maintain my composure though I was struggling with conflicting feelings of discomfort and sadness. 'Keep going,' I murmured.

'It's got a horrible ending, I'm afraid,' she said.

'I don't doubt it.'

'Well, the battle kept going all day, back and forth, back and forth, with men falling all around as they got shot, the wounded trying to crawl back . . .' She paused to take a deep breath. 'It wasn't until the next morning that Christiaan set out to find his two Roelofse kinfolk. He found my father first, with a bullet wound in his head. He was calling out for his grandson. Young WS was found close by, but he was dead. They carried the body across to my father, and with the boy in his arms, my father died.'

Linde brushed away tears. 'I am sorry, I am embarrassed. I haven't talked about it all to anyone for such a long time.'

I could feel tears pricking my own eyes. 'Don't be sorry, Linde. My God, what a sad story.'

'So, it's just me and Anja now. I cannot bear to call my husband's family kin and I am so lonely, Donald John.'

At this I put down the cart, walked over to her, put my arms around her, and hugged her tightly. As I stroked her hair she wept and clung tightly to me. Perhaps she saw me as something of a father figure, but to me, the embrace felt different. I wanted the moment to last far longer.

We resumed our journey. Linde's spirits gradually lifted and she regained the spring in her step. For a while I began to feel young again. The hours passed like minutes and the cart felt light. But later, as we grew tired, heavy rain came, and as we huddled under a cape, I thought of Morag and tried to banish all thoughts of Linde and that moment of intimacy from my mind. I was married: Linde would never be mine. Moreover, I was marching her towards a prison, and if the dreadful rumours were true, it was quite possible she and Anja would die there. I shuddered at the thought and knew I would do everything in my power to prevent their coming to harm.

Chapter 23

Donald John, Ardnish, 1944

'Look who I have here,' Angus announces, throwing open the door and grinning broadly.

Morag bustles in, then rushes around the room kissing everyone and replying to the stream of questions. 'Yes, I'm glad I went . . . Yes, I saw lots of my family I hadn't seen in ages . . . But wait, we'd better get organised. There's someone else coming here. I saw a man on the skyline.'

At last, she comes over to hug me. My heart swells with joy as she squeezes me tight. 'How did you get here so quickly?' I ask.

'There was an army officer on the train I got chatting to and he offered to take me up the loch in a boat. I was so relieved! Otherwise I would've been stuck at the Lochailort Inn until the thaw came!'

Mairi has gone outside to see who this stranger could be and returns a few moments later, a tall figure following her.

I'm astonished. I can scarcely believe what I am seeing, given that it has been just moments since I was thinking about his family. It is Archbishop Andrew himself.

Morag and Louise leap to their feet, but he motions them to sit down. 'Please! Stay where you are,' he insists. 'Canon MacNeil has a funeral on, and I thought I'd come myself.' He peels off his snow-covered coat, hat and scarf.

He turns to me. 'And how are doing, my old friend?' He takes my hand and shakes it firmly. We exchange a few pleasantries until a bout of coughing interrupts.

'Your Grace, some tea?' Morag asks.

'We'll not be having any *Your Graces* here, please,' he admonishes her. 'We're old friends.'

Morag swings into action immediately, resuming control of the household. She fusses around making the tea and putting drop scones on the griddle.

'How was your journey, Archbishop?' I ask. 'You must have got the early train. Morag has just arrived herself and – typical Morag! – persuaded a soldier to get a boat to bring her along.'

'I had a good walk over from Lochailort Station. I was surprised how deep the snow was, but it's crisp and bright outside, and I know the path well enough. There's deer everywhere. I saw a lovely stag right at the top, a royal at least. And an otter in the wee loch by the train line. The fresh air did me good.' He beams and sips his tea.

'You must be exhausted,' I say.

'Not a bit of it! Although I confess I haven't taken so much exercise in a long time. There were some mighty drifts I had to clamber through. I nearly headed down to Sloch at one point but I could see Roshven Hill to the south and remembered to keep left. I had a good tumble coming down that steep bank towards the big field!'

I smile. It is so typical of the Archbishop to make light of his trek.

'Canon MacNeil and I had a good natter with Iain Bec the train driver,' he continues. 'He dropped me off right at the bridge to save me the walk. It pays off, having a fellow Papist on the engine.' He chuckles. 'Anyway, Iain sends his best regards to you all and said he'd leave a sack of coal below the footbridge next time he comes through. Even if you can't retrieve it until the summer!'

'That's kind of him,' I say softly. We both know full well we are talking about something I shall not live to see.

'The train was full of youngsters, up doing training with the SOE at Arisaig House. Not just men, but women, too, I noticed.'

'Did you really come all the way from Roybridge just to see me?' I ask.

'I wanted to,' he replies straight away. 'Have we not known each other almost all our lives? In any case, Canon MacNeil has the big funeral at Polnish to attend to, so it suited everyone just fine.'

I feel my heart swell. He didn't have to do that. There can't be many people who have an Archbishop to hear their confession.

They all chat about this and that, and once we've establish that he will stay the night, everyone relaxes.

Mairi is keen to hear about Morag's trip. She never misses a good funeral herself, she'd be the first to admit.

'Well, it's certainly not how we'd do it here,' Morag says, inevitably. 'It was held at St Anthony's in Govan, where I used to go with my parents. I didn't know any of the hymns or the congregation other than my family. Maureen must have had lots of friends, though, as the place was packed, and we even went to a public bar afterwards.' She adds with mock surprise, 'Would you believe the place was full at four o'clock in the afternoon!'

Mairi shakes her head in disapproval though I see the Archbishop is smiling to himself.

'The priest was Irish,' Morag goes on, 'and I know for certain that he had three whiskies before I even finished my first. Father Declan, he was called. Do you know him, Archbishop?'

The Archbishop shakes his head. 'No, but I'll look out for him. There are quite a few Irish clergy in Glasgow who enjoy a dram.'

'How was the train?' Angus asks.

Morag smiles. 'The journey back was so beautiful. Coming through the old pine forest north of Tyndrum I saw two stags in the snow, right alongside the line on Rannoch Moor. And two red squirrels at Ardlui station! I knew you'd all be jealous when I told you that – we never see them up here. And the train guard pointed out a spot where there's an eagles' nest on the cliffs above Loch Treig.'

I look at my wife, holding the audience with her amusing tales of Glasgow and the wildlife she loves so much. As she talks, her hand fondles Broch's ears. The dog looks adoringly up at her. He's missed her, too. I do so love this woman, I think to myself. I need to tell her. It's years since I've uttered the words and I'd like her to know. My arms want to reach out and draw her towards me. I've missed her this past week and I was scared of dying before I could tell her what a fine wife and mother she's been. I need to say a proper farewell.

Chapter 24

Donald John, South Africa, 1901

Linde, Anja and I walked mile after mile of flat and characterless land, with only the occasional gazelle to be seen. There was precious little wildlife. The ground was the light brown of winter, in contrast to the waist-high bright green grass we had seen a few months ago. Now and again we would pass burnt-out farmsteads.

The number of British Army troops in the area was astounding, and we encountered many patrols marching or riding past every hour or so. We could see a long supply convoy in the distance and hear shelling from some distant engagement. There were around half a million men from all over the Empire in South Africa now. How could the Boer elude so many soldiers?

They were still creating quite a sting. Every day we came across torched army wagons, dead horses and scattered debris. You could smell the stench of the carcasses before you got close. Sometimes the Boer attacked at night, when the sentries were jittery, anticipating the enemy creeping into the camp in the pitch-black to slit their throats. Every whinny from a horse or shifting of stones beyond the camp perimeter resulted in a nervous call to 'Stand to!' and our precious sleep would be broken by an inevitable false alarm.

I was exhausted each night from pulling the cart and was always glad to turn in. As I lay wrapped up in my blanket, I would often pull out the letters from Morag, which I kept tucked in my tunic pocket. Her latest followed the usual script:

My dear DJ,
I was pleased to receive your letters – three arrived on the same day. I'm glad that you are likely to come home soon. Maybe it will be in time to help with the potato and turnip harvest. The children are being very helpful . . .

I was glad that Morag continued to write to me, but the letters were deflating; like this one, they were always strictly factual and lacking in intimacy. The excitement of the early days of our marriage was long past. My days back at home had involved digging ditches out in the rain, then coming back to a woman who didn't seem to need or want me any more. The war had definitely come along at the right time in many ways. The money was essential for my family's very survival at Peanmeanach, but it was clear that my absence wasn't making either of our hearts grow any fonder, and that saddened me.

I thought guiltily about Linde. I found myself constantly drawn to her. She was so pretty and vivacious when she laughed, it was infectious. Anja and I couldn't help but join in. I tried to put aside difficult thoughts of her going into a camp, and my wife, and my home, on those beautiful warm days. There was the distraction of sunshine, plenty of food, smiles and laughter, and knowing that there was still a week of trekking and chatting with this delightful woman. I admired her spirit, given what lay ahead. There was nothing that could be done to improve her situation anyhow, so I tried to make the best of it while it lasted.

I was keen to talk to her about Africa – the farming, what it was like to have servants, and why there were no giraffes, lions or elephants in this part of the country. But Linde kept questioning me. She wanted to understand the reasoning behind the land clearances.

'Do your generals not know what resentment this causes?' she challenged. 'The Boer will never give up the fight now! Their farms and livelihoods have been destroyed, their animals taken, their women and children imprisoned. They will fight to the death. If you gave fifty of your British pounds to every man you found at every farm instead, then the war would be over. Your men could return to their families and your country would be much richer.'

I couldn't fault her argument. I told her that land clearances had happened in the Scottish Highlands, and they, too, were unforgivable.

'When my cousin was a young man at Arisaig, a day's ride from my village, his family had the tenancy on a bit of land and a good number of cattle. His mother was a weaver. They were considered prosperous, but then Lord Cranstoun inherited the land from Clanranald's wife. Cranstoun lived far away in Berwick, over the Scottish border, but he wanted money from the estate and a substantial sheep farm, so the rents were increased by a huge amount. More than a hundred people from the areas on good land such as Ardnafuaran were unable to pay, so they were cleared off to poorer land on Ardnish. My cousin lived with us for a while before emigrating to Nova Scotia.'

I paused, knowing that some of these names would mean nothing to her. 'Do you really want to hear more about the troubles of people from the other side of the world?'

'Yes, Donald John,' she replied. 'I know so little of the rest of the world.'

'Well, back when I was in my twenties my father was called to give witness to the Napier Commission and I went with him. The point of this commission was that the landowners were driving folk off the good land so they could put their sheep there, and families were forced to move onto already crowded land or to emigrate, sometimes against their will, like the cousin I just mentioned.

'There were just too many people on poor land to survive. Smallpox killed many but the starvation was worse. On the Hebridean Islands, people stopped paying rent and began grazing their animals on the landowners' lands without authority. An organisation was set up called the Highland Land League to stir up resistance; they even sent men to Ardnish and encouraged us not to pay rent. I was a young man at the time, and I remember everyone in the village sitting around listening to what the rebel rousers had to say. Our decision was to do nothing as our landowner, a new laird, was doing his best to help us. But there really was a sense of revolt in many other places. It was a time of real turmoil across the Highlands.'

'So, do you rent your land?' Linde asked.

'We do. The families of Peanmeanach pay two pounds per annum and for that we can have three cows and twelve sheep per household, but we don't have that many as the ground wouldn't support it. Besides, we couldn't afford to buy more beasts. In the old days, the men from Ardnish were highly sought-after cattle drovers. They went over to the islands of Uist or Skye, and then worked their way south. They'd be away for a couple of months. Ronald the Bard was said to take cattle as far south as Wetherby in England, a journey of three hundred and fifty miles. He would play the bagpipes there and get good money for doing so. My father used to drove, too. I went with him a few times when I was young, taking herds of cattle from Lochaber down to Falkirk. In a single trip we would make fifteen pounds, but since the railway has come, that has stopped. The sheep and cattle are put onto trains at Lochailort now.'

'How else can you make money?' asked Linde.

'There's whelk-picking. It used to be good money in the winter, but now there are too many doing it, and there are not enough whelks to go around. It's horrible work, up to your knees in the sea in the depths of winter. You used to be able to earn a shilling and sixpence a day but now you'd be lucky to get a third of that. We get paid almost eighteen pounds a year in the army, so you can see what poor money whelk-picking is in comparison.'

Linde is thoughtful. 'And your landlord – you said he wasn't a bad man?'

'No, not at all,' I replied. 'Astley-Nicholson hasn't increased our rent, but it is such a lot to have to pay now that more families have moved over from Arisaig. We're all trying to survive on the same amount of land. Sir Arthur – he's the landowner – did have the idea at one time of starting a commercial business and giving regular work to men on the estate. He opened a peat works and eight men started on it. Peat was dug, dried out and bagged in hessian sacks before being put on a boat and sent to Glasgow. The laird was very pleased with his plan and the men were making a decent wage.'

'That sounds sensible,' Linde remarked.

'Well, the problem was that the men didn't want to be employed labourers. If it was a nice day they would take time off to go and cut hay, or thatch their houses. We Highlanders are an independent people. Everything needing done back at home was more important. One beautiful spring morning, Sir Arthur and Lady Gertrude took their infant son down to see how the men were doing, bringing bottles of cordial and cake, and they found not a single one of them there. The business lasted for less than a year before it was closed down.

'Sadly, many locals don't survive to old age. When I was born, there was a terrible blight on the potato crop and, at the same time, the herring numbers dropped. I remember my father telling me of visiting a house on the north side of Ardnish and finding a woman and her husband dead, skin and bone. They had died of starvation. And as if that wasn't bad enough, there wasn't enough milk for the children so there was a terrible occurrence of rickets on the peninsula. In fact, in my parents' day, as many children died as lived.'

Linde was aghast. 'Why did your family stay, then? Did things improve after the Commission? Did you lose any children yourself?'

Her questions came thick and fast, so fast that, mercifully, I didn't have to answer them all. Yes, Morag and I had lost two babies. It hurt my heart to recall it. I always wondered if her intense grief had made Morag a harder woman; the pain of it seemed to have made her withdraw into herself. She never shared her pain with me. I wasn't prepared to tell Linde any of this, though.

I changed the subject. 'Many of the people sailed from Arisaig to Antigonish and Mabou in Nova Scotia. The people there were our people; they spoke Gaelic and shared our way of life. Many also went to Australia, in search of an easier time, where a man could find work and food for his family, and the climate wasn't so harsh.'

Her face was a picture. 'How can it be so bad that people have to leave to survive?'

'Don't worry.' I smiled. 'My family has always managed better than most. There's a big mansion house, newly built across the bay, and every few years, the owners, a fine family called Blackburn, build onto it. I was the head joiner there and the pay is good. Mind you, that work is coming to an end now, because the Blackburns are old and have stopped the building work.'

I wanted Linde to know the reality of the West Highlands of Scotland as I saw it, and to make her understand why I would never leave. Yes, life was hard, but there was so much that was wonderful, too.

'I seem to have told you the very worst of it all. There are many good things, too!'

'It sounds like a struggle even to survive,' Linde whispered.

'Yes, it became that way. We desperately needed the army money.'

'I think you should come and live in South Africa.' Linde smiled shyly.

I caught my breath. Was I just imagining that she nearly added 'with me'? I continued. 'Linde, I want you to stop for a moment, and shut your eyes and visualise what I see when I go outside just after dawn and sit and drink tea outside my house.'

She did as I asked.

'In the spring, we always catch the first of the sun. The turf down to the beach is what's called machair, and the ground is ablaze with a multitude of tiny flowers. Beyond that, when the tide is out, acres of white coral sand squeaks and crunches when you walk on it. There is a pretty island in the foreground, covered with heather, and stunted trees that the deer haven't been able to get to. Then, a mile out across the sea, is a stand of pine trees and to the left of that is Roshven House – the one I was telling you about. There are two big hills, Rois-Bheinn and An Stac, that will still have snow on the peaks from the winter, and there often won't be a breath of wind after the gale of the previous day. The lambs will be calling to their mothers in the field behind the house and the hooded crows will croak as they soar above. I love the peace of that first waking hour,' I tell her. 'I've travelled a bit with the Camerons and Lovat Scouts, and I've yet to see anywhere that compares with my own country for beauty.'

She leant over and put her arm around my neck. 'It sounds special, Donald John ... beautiful.' Her eyes met mine, and I saw a tear on her cheek. I wiped it away with my thumb.

Suddenly, we heard a child screaming. We leapt to our feet.

'Anja!' Linde shouted as the distraught girl ran towards her and threw herself into her mother's arms. 'What is it, darling? Are you all right? Tell me!'

Anja was sobbing and gasping for breath, her words jumbled as she struggled to get them out. 'Hondjie is dead! Aunt Betje killed her with a knife!'

'No, Anja, that can't be possible!' Linde cried, her face flushed, blue eyes blazing in fury.

'It is, I swear! She told me that Hondjie attacked Pieter – but she didn't, Mother. Hondjie would never do that.'

Linde instantly stormed across the camp, Anja and I running to keep up. Two of the farm workers intercepted her, just feet away from where her sister-in-law was camped, and held her fast.

'You are a cruel and spiteful bitch, Betje!' Linde shouted as the woman emerged from her tent. 'Kill a little girl's dog, would you?'

The Boer woman drew her two children to her, a look of amusement playing on her face. 'The dog was about to attack Pieter. I had to do it.'

The women shouted back and forth: Linde aggressively berated her sister-in-law and the other tried to justify the animal's murder. A small crowd of soldiers and workers gathered.

Eventually I pulled Linde away. 'Nothing can be gained from this,' I said. 'Come on, Linde. Leave them alone.'

I led them away – Anja sobbing, her mother holding her tight – and went to find a shovel to bury Hondjie. My mind was whirring. Now I realised just how vengeful the family were and how deeply they hated her. I realised that her intimacy with me would allow them to justify attacking her, although they wouldn't dare do so with me and the other soldiers around. I would have to keep a close eye on all of them from now on.

Chapter 25

Donald John, South Africa, 1901

One day, Captain Willie caught me by surprise. He called me over, and I expected a friendly discussion about the progress of the convoy, but instead he let rip. His words are seared into my brain.

'I thought we had dealt with this, Gillies! Have you forgotten you're a married man? Damn it! You have children at home who depend on you, waiting for their hero father's return. And you, do you not value yourself more than this? You have a reputation second to none in Lochaber yet here you are, cavorting with a girl almost half your age, acting like a love-struck teenager. That girl is vulnerable, Gillies, and you are taking advantage of her. Shame on you!'

I was shaken by this attack and tried to defend myself, but he was having none of it. He dismissed me without allowing me to say a word. I stormed out, shaking with rage. I felt he was completely exaggerating the situation. Linde had saved my life, and I had not once acted inappropriately. This was how I rationalised the situation as I hurried straight back to the cart where Linde and Anja awaited my return. I could see Linde was puzzled by my angry expression, but I refused to answer her questions. Instead, I took myself away to a private spot and contemplated the sky as I tried to calm myself down.

Anja and I had become firm friends, which made me feel a strange mix of joy and guilt. I felt young again as we played games such as I-Spy together, and it was a distraction from the day-to-day drudgery of the convoy, the heat and the dust. At times I even verged on being openly insubordinate to Cammy and Captain MacDonald, such was my contentment when in the company of Linde and her girl. But as we got closer to Aliwal North, I became increasingly anxious about the prospect of leaving them there. I could no longer convince myself that the rumours surrounding the camps were exaggerated. It was now common knowledge that they were desperate places where sickness was rife, at the very least. I realised with alarm that the Vanloos women would tell others in the camp that Linde had befriended a British soldier, and I knew she would pay a high price for that.

The day before we were due to arrive at the camp there were long silences between us. We were both preoccupied with our own thoughts. My mind was racing. What would happen to Linde? To little Anja? Would I be able to keep seeing them? What could I do to help them? Their safety became my primary focus from then on.

I was aware of Linde's glances now and then. Something about her demeanour suggested that things were changing between us; when I met her gaze, she would bite her lip and look away. She must have been terrified of what lay ahead.

That evening we camped as normal in a vast *kraal*, with the women and children huddled around the fire in the centre for warmth and protection. The wagons were pitched in a circle outside that, and the horses and oxen tied up in lines to one side. We soldiers were on sentry duty, two hundred yards out, for four hours at a time. Before nightfall I walked past the civilians by the fire and noticed that Linde and Anja had been shunned by the others; they were sitting apart, leaning against a wagon. Linde saw me and gave me a little wave. There was something about the expression on her face that I couldn't get out of my mind. My body was aflame. I realised I hadn't felt so full of longing and passion for twenty years. I persuaded one of the Scouts to do my sentry duty and left to wash and smarten up. I planned to search her out in the middle of the night and nothing was going to stop me.

I decided to give it an hour until darkness fell and everyone was asleep, and then creep across to join her. I lay for ages, nervous as a teenage boy, summoning my courage and listening to the noises of the camp gradually quieten. I wanted to hold her close and whisper that I loved her. Did I dare to go further? To make love to her? It would be our only chance. It was time.

But at that very moment, just as I was ready to set off, Captain MacDonald came by with a lamp. 'Come on, Gillies,' he said. 'On your feet. We need to head out on patrol. There's a report of noise in the trees over there. Perhaps the Boer are coming to free their women. Get two other men to join us, and I'll be back in five minutes.'

I couldn't believe my ears. We'd be at Aliwal North tomorrow. I cursed once he was out of earshot, but I had no option: I had to follow orders. I was furious, until one of the corporals took me by my collar and hissed that I should behave myself. I shook him off.

The whole squadron of Scouts was being told to 'stand to'. We encircled the camp, silent men with loaded rifles, staring blindly into the darkness. Then our patrol headed off, blundering through the painful thorns that caught our clothes, up banks, along a dry riverbed for hours, stopping every few minutes to listen for the sound of feet or horses.

We must have been out for six hours, and our search was futile. If there had been Boer about, they would definitely have heard us and we would have been shot to pieces, I was certain. It seemed a highly unusual and unnecessary manoeuvre, and I couldn't get out of my mind that the whole operation had been instigated by the captain. I was so obsessed with my plan to reach Linde that I thought perhaps he'd guessed my intentions and wanted to put a halt to them.

It was still dark when we got back in. Silence reigned throughout the *kraal*. The camp had been stood down hours ago and we were told we had an hour to rest before breakfast. As I passed the back of an ammunition wagon, a shadow flitted out of the dark and tugged at my sleeve. It was Linde.

'You wanted to come to me last night, didn't you?' she whispered.

I couldn't speak, but nor could I lie. I nodded.

'I waited for you. I wanted you to come.'

Without a word I pulled her towards me and kissed her desperately, hungrily, giving in to the intense primal urge that had been building up over the past ten days. She was as frantic as me, her hands pulling at my hair, scratching my back, as our passion overtook our reason.

She stepped back. 'Under the wagon,' she gasped, pulling me down.

We scrambled underneath, disregarding the rocks and hard ground, and my right hand delved into her blouse to seek her breast while her hand struggled to undo my trousers. Our kissing was intense, each as passionate as the other.

Yet these nagging voices in my head would not stop. *This is madness. It's wrong. What about Morag? Linde is my prisoner. She's vulnerable . . . It's wrong!*

From close by, we heard a wailing voice. 'Mother! Mother!'

Linde froze.

'Mother! Mother!'

Anja was wandering around the camp crying out, increasingly desperately, for her mother. She was coming closer.

I slumped back and turned away.

Linde kissed me hard and whispered sorry before rearranging her dress and crawling awkwardly from our hiding place.

'What are you doing under there?' said Anja. 'Is that Donald John there, too?' Her voice was so piercing it seemed to echo round the camp.

And with that, mother and daughter, hand in hand, hurried away as I sorted out my clothing. I lay back, frustrated, eyes shut, hand on forehead, blood pumping. God, I needed that woman so badly.

Chapter 26

Donald John, Ardnish, 1944

The late afternoon passes in an amicable fashion. The Archbishop chats to me before he heads off with Morag to see the sheep and presumably listen to her opinion of what condition her husband is in. Angus spends his time helping around the place, doing the more strenuous tasks such as carrying peat and chopping kindling. Mairi fusses around like an old hen, dusting the dresser and sweeping the floor even though it doesn't need doing.

As dusk falls, with tea taken and the animals fed, everyone crowds around the fire. Morag helps me to sit up and arranges a blanket around my shoulders. She gives the Archbishop a full update on Donald Angus and Sheena, both of whom are in Canada. She loves telling visitors about the young. Louise constantly interrupts with additions to Morag's story, but they make a delightful team. They discuss the war and whether Churchill will be re-elected as prime minister, and the Archbishop tells us how he thinks Pope Pius is coping at the Vatican while Rome is being bombed by the Allies. It is pitch-black before we know it.

As they talk, I can feel the fluid in my lungs and become aware of an unpleasant gurgling as I inhale. Every breath is a struggle, and I interrupt the evening with a terrible fit of coughing, my body twisting and buckling. Louise holds a bowl under my chin as, finally, I vomit phlegm, crimson with blood. Afterwards I lie back, exhausted, my ribs aching and my body soaked in sweat from the exertion.

Morag holds my hand and looks deep into my eyes. 'Hold on, dear,' she whispers, dabbing my forehead with a handkerchief.

Mairi has returned from her house with fresh tea, using the chamomile she grows in a box on her windowsill. 'This will soothe him, help him relax,' she insists rather stridently to Louise, who, as always, looks sceptical whenever Mairi's potions are on offer. Unusually, Louise is in favour this time. She helps me to sit upright and plumps my pillows once more.

The Archbishop and my son are talking quietly in the background, no doubt about my final confession. I nod to myself, thinking it's long overdue.

Chapter 27

Donald John, South Africa, 1901

The Orange River was vast, bigger than the Lochy in spate and a deep burnt-orange colour from the red earth which prevailed in the area. At home we could look into a river and see a salmon ten feet below the surface, but here the water was muddy and clouded.

Off to our left, just out of sight, lay the concentration camp, the town of Aliwal sat in the middle, and to our right was the army camp, up on a hill. The vista stretched about three miles from one side to the other.

Captain MacDonald kept me with him all day. There always seemed to be some task or another that he needed me for. At several points I tried to break away to find Linde but I was always thwarted. He was watching my every move.

That afternoon, near the Frere Bridge, we had been waiting our turn to go across. To our amazement, a party of six British women approached us from behind. Captain MacDonald engaged them in conversation, and it transpired that they were an official party sent out by the British Government to report on the concentration camps, following the enormous hue and cry caused by the speech Emily Hobhouse had made in Parliament. Millicent Fawcett was one name I remembered. I overheard her saying that they'd just come from the camp at Bethulie and the camp here was one of the better ones. Apparently a genuine effort was being made to improve conditions.

The women were staying at the Royal Hotel in town and wanted to hear from us what had happened out in the veld when the Boer families were being escorted to the camp. We were invited to meet them at the hotel in a few days' time to give our account. I was encouraged by their words; these women had actually seen for themselves that conditions were becoming tolerable in the camps, and so, despite my sadness and frustration about my circumstances, my spirits lifted a little.

I managed to snatch a few minutes with Linde at dusk before I was due on sentry duty. I began to apologise profusely, stumbling over my words.

But she pressed a hand to my lips and spoke earnestly. 'No, no . . . please . . . don't say sorry. I know we'll soon be apart, and I wanted you too – just to hold you . . .'

'I am so glad to hear it. I was worried I . . .' I couldn't voice my feelings. 'Is Anja all right?'

Linde looked away. 'I don't think she really understood what was happening, but she was a little unsettled. She asked difficult questions. But, Donald John, I told her what a fine man you are and how you have been like a father to her these last few days – better than her own father ever was.'

I was deeply touched. I took her hand in mine, looked intently in her eyes and was about to tell her my feelings when I heard a bellow from Cammy, who must have been watching us from a distance. 'Corporal Gillies, get over here now!'

'That man has eyes in the back of his head,' I grumbled. 'I have to go, Linde. I'm sorry.'

Despite being on sentry duty for half the night, early the next morning I was sent on an errand to the town. I was to deliver a message to the commanding officer and return to the camp with post for the men. Dejectedly, I did as I was ordered, knowing that my precious final hours with Linde were being eaten away.

There was a letter for me, the address written in the instantly recognisable, neat hand of my wife. My heart sank as I slipped it into my pocket. My conscience was gnawing at me enough without reading a letter from Morag. What a day to get it!

Later that morning, a small group of Scouts, including myself, finally led the women and children towards the concentration camp. The chatter had stopped; even the youngest children seemed to sense that something bad was happening. They remained deathly quiet as their mothers held them close.

There were other Boer families being escorted to the camp, ahead of us and behind us, but only soldiers returning in the other direction, having completed their mission. I couldn't bear to look at Linde. I was still torn with remorse at what had taken place, but at the same time I felt an urgent need to take action. To save her. Perhaps if I could get hold of a couple of horses we could make a break for Basutoland – we were only a day's ride away, after all – but I felt powerless, exhausted. We were now within sight of the camp, and I stayed at the back of the group, suddenly aware of tears running down my face.

Anja appeared at my side and took my hand, then whispered in my ear: 'We need you, Donald John. You won't leave us, will you?'

I shook my head. 'No, I won't, Anja. You can rely on me.' I knew then that, whatever happened, I would never forget her words, the tone of her voice and her implicit trust in me.

At the gate we were introduced to Mr Greathead, the camp's commandant. At first glance the place looked better than a military camp: there were stalls selling food and clothing, a *kraal* for milk cows and a rudimentary school. Row upon row of neatly spaced white bell tents stretched into the distance. But despite Mrs Fawcett's reassuring words about the conditions, the lines of freshly dug graves alongside the river told another story.

Linde clung to me, silent, her eyes beseeching me not to leave her.

'I'll be back tomorrow,' I said firmly, trying to inspire confidence. 'I'll get you a mattress to keep you off the damp ground, and a paraffin cooker if I can.'

I turned and marched out of the camp. I couldn't bear to look back.

Later that day, we were reunited with the other Scout squadron. They'd been clearing farms, too, but from the east, and had been harried all the way in. At the battalion parade that night, the recently promoted Colonel Murray gave us the good news that the Second Contingent had landed in Cape Town. A week from now, they would be in Aliwal North. There was great excitement and cheering amongst the men. The colonel went on to inform us that after the hand-over Captain MacDonald would take our contingent by train to the Cape, and from there we'd sail to Southampton. Most of the regulars including himself, Lieutenant Macdonald and Captain Brodie of Brodie were to stay put. If any other ranks wished to remain for a further tour then they were to sign up now. I knew my duty was to return to my wife and family yet something was holding me back.

We were ordered to be on parade at seven in the morning for a trek to Zastron, from where it was believed General de Wet might be operating. We were to be accompanied by our comrades, the Connaught Rangers.

After dinner that evening, I finally opened the letter from my wife. Ardnish seemed to belong in another universe – a place remote and unreal. Morag's latest news, related in her matter-of-fact style, concerned the priest getting thrown from his pony and breaking his wrist, a flood and a thank-you for the five pounds I had sent, which meant they'd been to Arisaig and bought provisions for a month. For the first time she didn't describe the long list of tasks that awaited my return; there were no complaints and, to my surprise, even a line saying that she hoped I was safe and enjoying the excitement of the campaign. There followed an astonishing postscript: 'I miss you, Donald John, and count the moments until your return.'

This was quite unlike the dozen or so letters I had received since we'd been out here. It was almost as if Morag knew that my affections were being directed elsewhere. She signed off with the endearment 'God bless', which made me wince. God certainly knew all too well of my lust. Nervously, I dabbed beads of sweat from my forehead.

Donald Peter had enclosed a charming note, too; he couldn't wait for me to return and might I bring back an African spear and shield for his birthday? It made me laugh out loud until I felt a pang of guilt.

Our permanent new camp was comfortable enough. It had a canteen with decent grub and tents with mattresses. That night I lay in comfort but was unable to sleep as my mind raced with warring thoughts of my attraction to Linde and my wife and home. I got up and, sitting by a paraffin lamp, wrote to Morag, saying how much I was looking forward to coming back and seeing the family. I knew how much work there was to prepare for winter and I was ready to shoulder the burden. Bring the peat down to the village, dig the potatoes and turnips, go up to the loch above the house and cut reeds to repair the thatch; all that and more. Morag would be struggling to get it all done, even with the teenagers helping. I desperately wanted to see the children and lay thinking of them.

And Morag? Had I missed her, too? After the intoxicating trek I had just undertaken I felt unable – or unwilling – to answer my own question. Things had changed so much. *I* had changed. I felt restless and confused. I'd fallen for this vivacious, beautiful young South African woman – a woman who had courageously saved my life – and now she and her daughter needed my help. My decision whether to stay on in South Africa or return home could mean the difference between life and death for them. If I stayed out here I could visit them, take them provisions, make sure they got the best treatment in the camp, protect them. Yes, I would be away from Aliwal on active duty at times, but later, when things were resolved out here and the war was over, Linde would be safe again and settled somewhere. Then I could return to Ardnish. She'd easily attract another husband, someone who would look after her, I told myself, and I made myself believe it.

I thrashed around all night, wrestling with the choices. In the end it came down to the promise I had made to Anja: it couldn't be broken. I decided I would stay.

The next day was one of rest. I went to the quarter-master to get a replacement horse, and the morning was spent getting her shod and finding a saddle to fit. I signed the list of those volunteering to stay on, then rode to town and managed to get a cooker and mattress, at great expense. I then went straight back to the camp to find Linde. My heart was pounding at the prospect of seeing her again. It was only by telling the camp staff that I was delivering goods on behalf of Captain MacDonald that I was allowed in and it took me an age to find her accommodation.

I saw Anja first. She was playing draughts with stones, squares drawn in the dust. Then I saw Linde. She looked dreadful; her face was bruised and scratched, and she could only smile weakly as I squatted down beside her. She motioned that the rest of the Vanloos family were inside the tent. Anja sidled up to me and told me quietly that her mother had been attacked the night before.

Linde got to her feet, and we walked together along the row of tents, each with stoical women and their families sitting in silence outside.

I asked her to tell me everything.

'Betje was itching to humiliate me from the moment you left, Donald John. When we arrived at our tent, she intro-duced me to the women nearby as a whore and a traitor.

Then, when the food came around, she tried to take it all. Of course I wouldn't have that, and so both the sisters went for me.'

'I'll make these bitches pay,' I raged, making to head back to the tent, but Linde caught my arm.

'No! You can't help me by causing a fuss. The minute you go they will only attack me again. I daren't sleep. I need to protect my daughter.'

I reluctantly agreed to hold my tongue and went back with her into the tent. It smelled fetid and damp. Putting the bedding and cooker down, I realised it wasn't only the in-laws there; there were another three or four women and children seated in another corner. They shrank back when they saw me. I grabbed Linde's sister-in-law by the arms and shook her hard. 'You bitch!' I stormed, shaking off Linde's attempts to pull me away. 'You leave Linde alone or I'll come back and thrash you!'

Afterwards, my blood still up, I escorted Linde and Anja to the camp office where I asked to see Greathead. I showed him Linde's injured face and explained the threat she was facing. I pleaded that they be housed in a different tent, then, as he grew increasingly annoyed, started to rant at him. He told me that there were no other tents available at present but more were expected soon, and he would see what could be done.

Linde was furious with me. 'You're just making it worse for us! You should never have come!' she cried.

I was told to leave the camp immediately and had no choice except to obey. After I was escorted outside the perimeter, I spoke to her through the fence. I knew she was right and I mumbled an apology. They stood, looking terrified, gripping onto the wire, their faces streaming with tears.

'I have to leave with the unit on a trek tomorrow,' I told them. 'But I'll be back, I promise.'

Kicking myself for my outburst, I decided to return after the mission to Zastron. I hoped that perhaps Captain MacDonald would soften his stance a little on hearing this predicament, come with me and help sort things out. I was nervous about seeing him as I knew he would be angry with me. My signing on for a second tour despite my family responsibilities at home would undoubtedly displease him.

As I rode back into the town, I observed a group of dejected families being escorted along the riverbank towards the camp. It was a beautiful winter's afternoon, and I should have been enjoying the glorious sunshine and excited about going home. Instead I was staying here, depressed and wracked with guilt. What was I doing?

When I got back, I went about my usual chores, including taking hot water to the captain for him to shave. He told me that our meeting at the Royal Hotel with the British delegates was arranged for four o'clock. I was delighted, hoping that this time together would provide an opportunity to have a quiet word with him about Linde and Anja.

The hotel was beautiful, not unlike the Station Hotel in Inverness or the Lovat Arms in Beauly. I marvelled at the carpets and chandeliers when I walked in; it was all such a contrast to the basic tents I had grown used to. Captain MacDonald had already arrived and was drinking tea with the ladies when I joined them. Rather than hearing the encouraging reports I had been expecting, Mrs Fawcett was most distressed by what she had witnessed at the camps. She told us that the water was polluted and there was no fuel for the women to boil water or cook the raw meat and vegetables they had been provided with. When they were at Bethulie it had been very wet and the mud floors of the tents were under three inches of water. Typhoid, whooping cough and measles were rife, and the site was indescribably unsanitary. With around five thousand people interred in the camp, there were very few medics and some of them had taken to misusing the alcohol intended for treating ailments. Mrs Fawcett held back tears as she recounted her experience, especially concerning the starving children. 'They die, almost all of them. They lie limp and fade away in their mothers' arms.'

I listened in silence, aghast.

'It's not that the camp staff are cruel,' she continued. 'It's that they lack the most basic things: proper latrines, clean water, disinfectant soap. Those could save thousands of lives. Emily Hobhouse made this very clear nine months ago and it's only just now beginning to take effect. But not nearly quickly enough, I'm afraid to say.'

Of course, with every word Mrs Fawcett said, I was thinking of Linde and Anja. Would those Vanloos women let her have the paraffin cooker to boil water? Would they steal her bedding and restrict her food? While Captain MacDonald was talking privately to Mrs Fawcett, I took one of the other ladies aside and told her about Linde. I asked if she might visit her and see if she was all right. Perhaps she could check that Linde still had the cooker I'd given her, that she was getting clean water and, hopefully, arrange to have her and Anja moved to a different tent away from her in-laws. The lady nodded and said she would see what she could do, though I detected a raised eyebrow. I had no doubt that my fretful concern revealed the reason for my remonstrations.

Captain MacDonald mentioned the rumours in the camps – and in the press – that the British were putting ground glass in the food. The ladies confirmed that they had heard this story, too, but, they explained, it was not ground glass at all. Potassium permanganate, in the form of Condy's crystals, was being added to the tinned food to make it last longer. The rumour had been started by the Boer to stir up hatred of the British Empire and highlight their plight.

As we headed back up the hill to the camp, Captain MacDonald rounded on me the moment we were alone. 'Gillies, I gather you have put your name on the sheet to stay out. Well, your request has been turned down. You are sailing back with the rest of us after Zastron, and that is the end of the matter. I don't wish to discuss it any further.'

I started to make my case, reminding him what he had heard about the death rates in the camps and that I couldn't simply abandon Linde and Anja. I tried to tell him how Linde had saved my life, but he wasn't prepared to listen to a word and stormed off ahead.

Chapter 28

Donald John, South Africa, 1901

What was expected to be our final week on active service was not a successful one. Alongside the Connaught Rangers, we rode on our mission to Zastron, which took two days. We found out where the De Wet Commando had been just one day before, and rode all the way back having achieved precisely nothing. The Boer were such experts at slipping away. They always had pickets out, sometimes as far as ten miles away from their encampment, and thus had plenty of warning of our approach. A guide once told us that the British Army were like a herd of charging elephants and the Boer were like cunning leopards. It felt like trying to catch trout with my hands in the burn at home. Perhaps De Wet had disappeared into Basutoland as it was so close to Zastron. I could see its beautiful, snow-capped mountains, thousands of feet high, in the distance.

Throughout the futile trek I continued to fret about Linde and Anja. Were they being bullied? Did Mrs Fawcett secure them a different tent? Clean water? Were they surviving the harsh conditions? I pictured Linde in my mind: her long fair hair and delightful smile, the laughter we'd shared during our time together despite the circumstances. I tried to recall her reaction when my hand was on hers, or when I took my handkerchief and gently wiped the sweat and grime from her face. I knew that she was as attracted to me as I was to her and I longed to be alone with her again. If only Anja hadn't interrupted us as we had lain beneath the wagon! Although Captain MacDonald had done everything he could to keep us apart, my passion remained as strong as before.

The keener I was to get back to Aliwal, the slower our convoy seemed to become. First, the girth broke on my saddle and I had to use a pair of trouser braces to tie it together, and then we had to take a detour to a farm that we spotted in the distance. It hadn't been burned down, but as soon as we reached it we could tell that no one was there. As I walked through the rooms I could see that the farmers had fled as dinner was being prepared. A horde of flies buzzed around mouldy vegetables and a rotting chicken. The beds were made up and looked inviting. I imagined Linde and me there, entwined, with all the time in the world and no one else within miles. Then, just a few miles away from Aliwal, we were delayed for a whole day after unusually heavy rain caused us to be stuck on the wrong side of a swollen river.

To pass the time, the talk amongst the men was all about getting home to the Highlands and their excitement about seeing the women in their lives. Cammy and I talked about having a big reunion in December at the Volunteer Arms in Fort William, and all the Lochaber men were keen to come.

In the final hour of the trek Captain MacDonald came over to me and we rode together. I expected to get another lecture from him about my behaviour, but instead we talked about the horses: how they were in such poor condition, exhausted and suffering from various ailments after their exertions. Many had shed shoes and were limping badly. We hoped that the Second Contingent would have reached Aliwal North by the time we arrived, so we could head down to the Cape as soon as we had handed over the horses and firearms. He did not mention my previous insubordination and my request to stay out longer. I was surprised by his lack of censure at first, but later I suspected that, after his order to sail back with the First Contingent, he believed I wouldn't see Linde again and that disaster had been averted.

Chapter 29

Donald John, Ardnish, 1944

A wave of chatter about Angus's ordination party has started up. I love to hear the merriment but I need to be alone with the Archbishop now. 'Would you, please, listen?' I say, as firmly as I can, to break the flow. 'I want to have a talk in private with the Archbishop, so if you could all have supper tonight at Mairi's that would be grand.'

Louise is remonstrating at the party being broken up and Mairi is muttering that she still has some fish pie left, but they all know why and dutifully get up. I can hear my wife saying to the Archbishop in a hushed tone that if I start to fade, he must come and get her.

'Of course he will, Mother,' says Angus. 'Archbishop Andrew knows where we are. Come.'

The three women and Angus put on their coats, and Morag crosses the room to kiss my forehead.

Finally, we have the house to ourselves. The Archbishop stokes the fire – I observe the care with which he handles the crumbly peat – and then he comes to my bedside, adjusts my pillow and sits down. He waits for me to speak.

'Archbishop,' I begin awkwardly, 'I've been living with a secret for some forty years and I need to get it out before I go. It's about a woman. I was your brother Colonel Willie's piper and batman, as you know, at the time. He knew about it.' I pause, staring into the fire.

The Archbishop nods. 'Go on. I'm listening.'

'I want to tell you everything, to get it off my chest – my last confession,' I say, anxiety fluttering in my chest.

He rises, crosses the room and retrieves a half-bottle from his bag. With a twinkle in his eye, he fetches a couple of glasses. 'It helps to have a parishioner amongst the excise men,' he murmurs, pouring two measures. 'This will maybe help you to remember the details, Donald John.'

I am delighted. It's months since I had a sip of the blessed *uisge beatha*. I swirl it around the glass, draw it into my nose, savouring the aroma. I touch the moisture against my lips, a drop, just a drop; it has to last the night.

There is a long silence as he waits for me to begin; only the wind whistling outside and the rhythmic tick of the clock on the dresser can be heard.

I meet his gaze. 'I am ready.'

The Archbishop drapes his stole around his neck and, murmuring '*Munire me digneris*', puts his cross over his neck. 'Take all the time you need,' he says gently. 'And tell me everything.'

'Bless me, Father, for I have sinned,' I whisper. And then, squirming uncomfortably at the realisation, I add, 'It's ... forty-seven years since my last confession.'

Chapter 30

Donald John, South Africa, 1901

When we finally reached Aliwal North, the Second Contingent were waiting for us: fresh-faced lads, many of whom were friends and relations of our men. We were instructed to hand over our rifles and horses to them and depart within an hour as the train was already loaded with others and waiting for us. If we missed the ship from Cape Town, no one knew how long it would be before we could get another. We were told we could sleep on the train and that there would be a big breakfast ready for us the next morning. No one complained and spirits were high; we were homeward bound.

But my stomach churned. Just three miles away were Linde and Anja, and they were undoubtedly suffering. How could I do this to them? How could I abandon them without saying farewell? I couldn't just tear myself away. They needed me. Linde was clearly in danger and I had made a promise to Anja.

It seemed, in that frantic hour of upheaval, that the captain's eyes were always upon me. We gathered at the station where Captain MacDonald carried out the roll call.

'Black Sandy, Mull River? Macdonald Seventeen? Sergeant Cameron? Piper Gillies?'

'Here, sir!' I called out in response.

We climbed on board the train, settled into our seats, and the whistle blew. The train juddered, and we watched the eager faces of our replacements recede into the distance. The mood was jubilant and the weariness of the last few days melted away as the men talked excitedly. Captain MacDonald walked through the train. He caught my eye and I lifted my hand in acknowledgement.

'Home soon, Gillies,' he said, smiling.

I sat there in silence, my head against the window, feigning sleep, in my own private world. Linde would be devastated by my betrayal, my disappearing without a word, and Mrs Fawcett's warnings about the camps were ringing in my ears.

Seconds later, my mind switched to Morag, standing outside the house at Peanmeanach as I left, the sun behind her. We'd spent twenty-two years together since we made our marriage vows. *For better or for worse.* All marriages went through bad patches, but perhaps things would be better once I got home. After all, her letter had made it clear she missed me and wanted me back home with her.

I closed my eyes. I had betrayed my wife and I was probably condemning Linde and her child to death. I had broken God's commandments. I was a wretched man. I crossed myself and prayed for Mother Mary's guidance. 'Hail, holy Queen, Mother of mercy, hail, our life, our sweetness, and our hope. To thee do we cry . . .'

One by one, the men were lulled to sleep by the rhythm of the train. I gazed into the darkness, the black sky with an occasional flash of distant lightning. It must have been about two hours since we had left. I was aware of the train slowing to a halt. We were arriving at Burgersdorp. Every mile was taking me further and further from Linde and Anja and their fate.

I made my decision. I rose from my seat and the movement stirred Cammy, who was dozing on the seat opposite. 'What are you doing?' he asked blearily.

'I'm going back, Cammy. I have to make sure Linde is safe. Will you tell Captain MacDonald, please? But not until tomorrow.'

Cammy blinked. 'You're staying?'

'Yes,' I replied, unable to meet his eyes.

'But what on earth will you say to Morag?'

'That's my concern.' I could feel my cheeks burning as I spoke.

Cammy wasn't impressed. 'My God, man – don't be so rash! Think of your family!'

But my mind was made up. I held out a case. 'Here are my bagpipes. You know how precious they are to me. Will you please take them back and leave them in the Highland Bookshop in Fort William? I'll pick them up when I get back.'

He shook his head but stowed the pipes with his belongings.

I jumped off the train and moved quickly into the shadows. Luckily, everyone seemed to be asleep. No windows were open, and I could see only Cammy's worried face pressed against the glass. I waved at him as the train gathered pace and disappeared from sight.

I was alone.

I knew there would be a hell of a to-do in the morning. Captain MacDonald would be furious and would undoubtedly charge me with being absent without leave. I was now a deserter. I was at risk of being court-martialled and shot.

I slumped against the station building. It was too late now: I'd made my decision. At dawn I would climb on a train going north and head back to Aliwal. I would find Linde, check that she and Anja were safe and had basic provisions, and then I would turn myself in to Colonel Murray.

But the very first thing I had to do, as soon as I got back to Aliwal, was to get to the Royal Hotel, sit down and write to Morag, and make sure the letter went in the post. I had written to her only days ago to say how pleased I was to be returning soon, and I knew that she and the children would be excited. She would be upset when she discovered I wasn't returning when I said I would be, although not as upset as she would be if she knew the reason behind it.

It was a long, cold night without a blanket, but I was so mired in gloom I doubt I would have slept in any case. Although I was fearful, I didn't regret for a second my decision to turn back.

The next morning, I bought a bowl of mealies from a stall and sat waiting for a train. Several passed, with blasts of their whistles and clouds of smoke: an armoured train bristling with guns; several hospital trains heading south; and one crammed with women and children bound for the concentration camp at Bethulie. I prayed that these poor souls were unaware of the conditions Mrs Fawcett had told us about. The women's eyes stared at me with hostility; the children, oblivious, were playing and chatting happily. I realised it was probably their first time on a train.

It wasn't until midday that I finally boarded a train. It was full of fresh recruits heading to Bloemfontein and a smattering of British civil servants heading beyond to Pretoria. I avoided conversation apart from explaining to one persistent individual that I was carrying a message on behalf of my commanding officer. There seemed to be no limit to the amount of deceit I was now engaged in.

Later, in the hotel lounge at Aliwal, I sat chewing my pen, an uneaten beef sandwich in front of me, wrestling with how best to tell Morag that I wasn't going to return as planned.

Royal Hotel,
Aliwal North,
OFS, South Africa

15th July 1901

Dear Morag,

I write this letter with a tortured heart, knowing what distress it will cause you. I have decided to remain in Africa for a while, and am signing up for a further tour with the Second Contingent, who have just arrived.

There remains much work to do here and I would like to see it through. I have also made a promise to someone and I cannot renege on it.

I know you will be struggling with the harvest now. I am very sorry not to be helping. Please take some comfort that the money I am saving is substantial. It will look after us well and we will be able to buy a few more sheep when I return.

Give my love to Angus, Sheila and Donald Peter. I miss them.

I believe the campaign has not long to run and promise to you that I will be home before long.

Your husband,

D. J. Gillies

I nearly signed off with 'yours faithfully', but, blushing, could not write the words. I handed the letter to the concierge for mailing, paid him for the postage and left the hotel.

It was an hour's walk to the camp, and I passed a stream of people on the route. At times I almost broke into a run, so keen was I to see her.

Remembering my run-in with the camp commandant, I knew I'd have to avoid the main entrance. I climbed through the barbed wire and scurried along the riverbank, in full view. I rushed around, peering in tents, expecting the camp staff to come running at any moment.

When I finally set eyes on her, I didn't get the reception I was hoping for.

'Donald John,' she said, not even getting up to greet me. She looked more cross than pleased. 'What are you doing here?'

'Oh, Linde,' I said. 'I'm so sorry I left.' I squirmed uncomfortably. 'I've come to help you. Is there somewhere we can talk?'

We walked along the riverbank. The flimsy fence between us and freedom felt absurd. Anja trailed along behind. I squatted down and encouraged her to come forward for a hug but she hung back, behind her mother's skirts. Her face was paler than I had ever seen before and she had dark shadows under her eyes, as did her mother.

I told Linde how I'd jumped off the train to come and look for her, how she and Anja really mattered to me, and that I wouldn't rest until I could get them out of the camp. I'd get medicine and find a room in the town for them to stay in. My rush of promises tumbled awkwardly over themselves. In reality I had no idea what I could do to help and I could see Linde knew that.

The whole encounter was awkward and tense. A British soldier making a social call on a Boer woman understandably drew a great deal of attention. We returned to the tent and sat on our haunches outside, in full view of the others, who were all shooting dark glances at us. Linde had been assigned a different tent, though, away from her relatives, which she thanked me for. That made me relax a little. She explained that Mrs Fawcett and her ladies had organised it, although her mother-in-law had kept the paraffin stove. She told me that there had been another fight at the water pump the previous day. Betje had been there, and had started berating her loudly.

'Here's the whore, sleeping with a British soldier, telling him our secrets! She's a traitor, she should be executed!'

Linde had fled, face crimson with shame.

'I'll go and sort this out once and for all,' I exclaimed, rising to my feet.

Linde grabbed my hand and pulled me down. 'No! You will not. Don't come again, Donald John, please,' she pleaded. 'It only makes things worse for us. The word will spread that you have been in the camp, and then the other women in the tent will tell the camp staff. We will be given half-rations. Anja is sick and hungry, and I cannot bear to see her suffer any more. You must understand.'

Despite her remonstrations, I vowed to return the next day. I'd bring coal so she could boil water, and some soap. She clutched my arm. 'Unless you can get us out of here for good, don't come back, Donald Angus.'

As I made my way back to the town my mind began to formulate all sorts of wild plans. Linde was terrified of reprisals. Anja had been listless, had barely acknowledged me. It was as though she had resigned herself to the worst. I had bought an expensive tin of Queen Victoria chocolates for her, but she'd barely glanced at them. She was a far cry from the chatty, lively lass I'd played with on the veld only days before. How could I get them out? Maybe I could find an abandoned farm. There must be one or two on the way to Zastron where we could take cover. I'd need two horses, some civilian clothes, food and various other basic necessities. But the veld was teeming with soldiers from both sides. The Boer and the British would want to hunt us down. It seemed hopeless, but surely this bloody war must be coming to an end. Was it just a matter of time?

I checked in to a guesthouse on the main street, which was run by an elderly couple. The husband was an Englishman, his wife a black African. Anticipating some searching questions from him, I gave a false name and explained that I was there on behalf of my colonel. I had been authorised to take lodgings rather than stay in the camp overlooking the town. I wasn't sure he believed me, but fortunately he couldn't be bothered to question me. He told me that he and his wife were the only mixed-race couple in the town and the locals didn't talk to them.

The next day I trudged back to the camp with a sack of coal over my shoulders. I fully expected to incur Linde's wrath for showing up without a plan to take her and Anja away, but Mrs Fawcett had said that not being able to boil water to get rid of germs was the primary cause of death in the camps, and of course they needed fuel to cook the vegetables and meat. I decided to risk Linde's anger if it meant keeping her alive.

At the gate I was quizzed about my business by a couple of sergeants. I gave a vague description of how I'd brought in a Boer family from their farm a few days ago and was just delivering some coal for them to cook with. Grudgingly, they let me pass.

Inside, however, a reception party was waiting for me: the adjutant and Sergeant Mackenzie. I was told brusquely to put down the coal, get on the spare horse they'd brought, and immediately return to camp with them, where I'd be in for a dressing-down by the commanding officer. My plea to allow me to deliver the coal fell on deaf ears. As we rode along, Sergeant Mackenzie told me that a telegram had been sent from further down the railway line informing them that I'd absconded and giving details of exactly where they would find me. He told me I would very likely be court-martialled.

I grew increasingly distraught at the realisation that all my efforts to help Linde had failed; in fact I'd caused her more problems. I suspected she'd never get the coal. I'd been a fool. My plan to get horses and for us to make a run for it was ridiculous. My bid for freedom had lasted forty-eight hours, and I was now in a great deal of trouble. Yet all I could think of was how I could let Linde know what had happened and reassure her I'd be back to rescue them.

I stood to attention in front of Colonel Murray. He delivered a furious and deserved reprimand, but he also acknowledged my hitherto unblemished record and noted that he knew Captain MacDonald would wish him to recognise this.

Before he sentenced me, he asked if I had any extenuating circumstances. I requested a private hearing, and the adjutant and sergeant were dismissed. I poured out my heart to the colonel, describing in detail how Linde had deliberately knocked old Mr Vanloos' rifle out of the way, thus saving my life, and how I felt responsible for this vulnerable woman and young child who had come to depend on me. I was convinced that their only hope for survival in the camp was with my help, and I couldn't walk away and let them die. I spoke from the heart and I could see his attitude soften.

'What exactly did you think you could do to help?' he enquired.

'Being able to boil water is crucial to keeping these people alive, yet they have no fuel, no coal. The water is polluted. My mind was full of crazy plans, but nothing seemed to work out . . . I've made a right mess of things, I know it. I really have.'

'It certainly looks that way,' the colonel agreed.

'To be honest, sir, I've come to realise that I've only been making things worse for the woman; the others in the camp attack her because of me.' I paused, sensing an opportunity. 'Might you be able to help, sir? Get them released? Perhaps you could save their lives.'

'I cannot, I'm afraid, Gillies,' he replied gently. 'One cannot order the release of individual detainees because of personal pleas. That's the end of it.'

'Please?' I pleaded. 'Is there *nothing* that can be done?'

It was some time before the colonel spoke again. 'Gillies,' he said at last, 'I find your intentions honourable, but as you are well aware you have shown a blatant disregard for military discipline. There will be a further hearing, and I should warn you that a court-martial is likely.'

'Yes, sir,' I said, head bowed.

'In the meantime, you will be demoted to Private with immediate effect and placed under the orders of Sergeant Mackenzie.' I turned to leave, but he wasn't done. 'Gillies, you should know that I will not attempt to defend the concentration camps; they are abhorrent. I will personally ensure that the quartermaster arranges for coal to be delivered to the camp for cooking and ensure that everyone receives a fair share. That is something that *is* within my powers. Dismissed.'

Chapter 31

Donald John, South Africa, 1901

The recently arrived Scouts, some of which were close friends of mine, gave me a good-natured welcome back at the camp. They'd heard I was getting hauled over the coals, although they didn't know the details. There were some Lochaber men amongst them and I was conscious that word of my activities out here might get back home. I tried to make light of the whole situation.

Sergeant Mackenzie came by as we turned in. 'I'll be watching you, Gillies. Just you stay where you are,' he said with a wink.

Despite my cheerful facade, I was in utter despair. I tossed and turned, still wondering whether I could steal some horses at first light and gallop down to the camp and spirit Linde and Anja away. It wasn't until the small hours that I drifted off into an uneasy sleep.

The new recruits were clean-shaven, in smart new uniforms. First Contingent took a lot of ribbing for looking like the Boer Commando, what with our long beards, ammunition belts draped over our shoulders and hats like those the Boer wore. Lord Lovat was back out again, although this time commanding the Second. I was assigned to be with Captain Edward Murray, a Cameron officer who had just arrived and bore no relation to our commanding officer, who was also staying out in South Africa.

We soon discovered that the Second Contingent had undertaken very little preparation. Many had undergone only an intensive week's training at Macrae and Dick's riding school in Inverness. Six shepherds had brought their collies out to help round up the sheep when clearing farms, but unfortunately the dogs always ran away when we were under fire.

The following night was bitterly cold. As I sat by the fire, I thought how wrong it was that we were chucking lumps of coal on it when only a few miles away that same coal would have saved lives.

Suddenly we heard a horse galloping into camp at full tilt. We leapt to our feet, instantly alert. It was a Connaught Ranger, demanding to know where the CO was. We were soon informed that the Connaughts were under attack and in dire straits a thirty-mile ride away. A long night in the saddle proved to be an agonising experience for many of the new recruits, who were just off the ships and hadn't ridden at all since they'd left Inverness weeks ago.

By the time we reached the location, the Boer outposts had seen us coming and vanished. We arrived to find six dead Connaughts and many wounded. The surviving men were all parched, having long since run out of water, and they had almost no ammunition left. For two days they'd been taking cover behind boulders on the *kopje*, with no escape from the sun. If we Scouts hadn't come to the rescue there would have been massive Connaught casualties.

Over the last few months of the war the Scouts and the Irish often camped and fought alongside each other, and many firm friendships were formed. As I helped to patch up the wounded before the doctor and hospital wagons arrived, I recognised one of the injured, Danny O'Driscoll from Tipperaray. Danny had taken a bullet in his stomach and was in agony. One of the new officers had brought his own supply of morphine and a syringe from Britain, and he allowed one of our lieutenants to give Danny a shot. Danny wanted to dictate a letter to his wife, so Colonel Murray's batman gave me a pencil and paper. I wrote as he spoke his heartfelt words of love, promised to post it, then gave him his last rites as the doctor appeared. There was nothing he would have been able to do anyway. I was holding Danny's hand as he breathed his last.

There were six hundred men clustered on that small hill. We worked hard, digging graves and transporting the many injured to the wagons. The Connaught Rangers' priest stood on a knoll and said the funeral Mass. We all knelt before him, hats and rifles by our sides. I wished I'd had my pipes with me as the bodies were laid in their shallow rocky graves. I would have played 'Flowers Of The Forest', the most moving of all laments. There was no wood for crosses, just waist-high cairns constructed by the soldiers to mark each man's resting place.

Our journey back was slow and laborious. The Indian medical service had supplied the stretcher bearers and medical staff, and wagons painted with red crosses. Their oxen travelled at a rate of a mile an hour, and every channel in the veld was a major obstruction that needed to be negotiated. Food and water were in very short supply, and the horses were still recovering from the fast ride out. I frequently dismounted and led my horse to give her a rest and to stretch my legs. Some of the new men were very hard on their mounts and wondered why they couldn't keep going. The Second Contingent had had a hard introduction to the war.

By the time we got back in we had been away almost a week. I had spent a lot of time praying that things might be better for Linde and Anja, and I was relieved to hear that Mrs Fawcett had appointed a matron and the military had agreed to help the civilian staff to improve conditions. I was convinced that Linde would be thinking I'd taken her at her word and just washed my hands of the two of them.

I was confined to camp, but I had to see her. I rose before dawn and slipped away on foot, running as fast as I was able. I reckoned I could make it to the camp and back before anyone noticed I'd gone. When I arrived, there was a stranger at the gate and he let me in without question. With mounting trepidation, I walked down the row of tents to the far end.

When I arrived at the tent I pulled back the canvas flap and peered in. Several women looked up at me. I saw Linde's cape on the mattress in the corner, the tin of chocolates, empty, beside it.

'Where is Linde?' I asked.

An old woman stared blankly in my direction. 'She died, this morning.'

I felt as if I might collapse as her words sank in. *Dead . . . this morning.*

'And Anja,' I asked hoarsely, 'her daughter?'

'At the infirmary.'

Anja was lying curled up on a mattress, only a mass of dishevelled blonde hair visible above the thin sheet. I knelt beside her and took her hand. She wasn't moving, but I could detect a faint pulse. I turned her over as gently as I could. Her beautiful face was a ghastly shade of grey, masked with a sheen of sweat. She opened her eyes, focused and then held out her hands, murmuring my name.

I held her in my arms for a long time, feeding her mealies on a teaspoon, stroking her hair, talking nonsense, caressing her cheek – all the time willing her to live. My mind darted between uncontrollable grief and wondering what had happened.

It grew dark. There was no one else around and just a dim lamp in the corner. Mrs Fawcett arrived with the camp matron and spotted me. She knelt down and took Anja's pulse. 'I think she'll live now,' she said.

'What happened to them? I asked.

'There was a commotion down by the river,' the matron replied. 'We heard screams, so I ran down with two of the nurses, but we were too late. Linde had already drowned, and Anja must have run in to help her. She was caught in the current and swept downstream. We found her some distance away, unconscious on the riverbank. We had to pump water out of her chest.'

'Linde drowned?' I said, perplexed. 'But how on earth . . .'

'The women at the river slipped away as soon as we arrived. They said they saw the woman and her daughter drowning and had gone to save them.'

'Was it her family?' I demanded, suddenly enraged.

The matron shrugged her shoulders. 'Perhaps,' she replied. 'Whatever happened or did not happen, we will never be able to prove anything. Not in here.'

My knees buckled as the reality hit me. Linde was gone, and I knew I had played a role in her death.

'What will happen to Anja now?' I asked weakly.

'In the normal course of events, the child would be adopted by her next of kin, which in Anja's case is her aunt. She's here in the camp.'

The matron could see the look of horror on my face.

'But she was one of the people who just tried to drown her mother,' I spluttered. 'You know it's true.'

'I don't know any such thing,' she said sternly.

'Oh yes, you do,' I retorted. 'You were aware of the bad feeling between them, weren't you?'

Mrs Fawcett spoke up. 'Please, don't worry. We'll look after her. There is a young couple in the town who have recently lost their only daughter, and I'm certain they would take her in and be good parents for her. I had intended to visit them this evening.

'I'm sorry this has been such a shock for you. Why don't you write the girl a letter? I'll make sure she gets it in due course. It will matter to her as she grows up.'

I took the paper and pen she offered and sat down to write. I proceeded to pour out my affection for them both, describing how much I had loved her mother despite only knowing her so briefly, and said I would pray for them every day for the rest of my life. I addressed it 'to my darling Anja' and sealed the envelope.

Mrs Fawcett took it and assured me that she would look after Anja. I went over to the child one more time. She was sleeping, breathing evenly; her fever had passed. I kissed her hand and then slipped away. I was relieved to know that Mrs Fawcett was taking responsibility for the girl's wellbeing. I knew I could trust her to do the best for Anja.

I thanked the two women and headed back to the camp, knowing there would be hell to pay. Nervously, I reported straight to Colonel Murray's tent and asked his orderly if I could have a word. I was prepared for the worst, having deserted not once but twice. It wasn't the glorious end to my army career that I had envisaged.

Sitting at Colonel Murray's desk, I related the events of the last few hours, and his stony face began to soften. When I had finished, he smiled. 'You're a very fortunate man, Gillies. With so much going on here, I don't have time to worry about such personal affairs. And, sadly, it's clear you won't need to go back to the refugee camp any more.'

My eyes welled up.

He got out of his chair, put a hand on my shoulder, looked me in the eye and said, not unkindly, 'Now, let's get back to soldiering, shall we?'

Chapter 32

Donald John, Ardnish, 1944

It is well past midnight, and I've been drifting in and out of consciousness, sometimes talking to the Archbishop, sometimes just dreaming. Our conversation roams back in time to how our families met.

'Your great-grandfather and mine would have been shepherds and drovers for the legendary Corriechoillie,' I tell him, guiltily delaying the confession of my greatest secret.

'Yes, that's right,' he replies, 'and later my grandfather, Long John, got his licence to become a legal distiller and began to build his whisky company.'

'You must be about ten years younger than me. Would that be right?'

'I'll be seventy-four next month. But I feel well on it.'

We pause for a moment, both deep in thoughts of the past. I am a very old man, that is certain. I can't think of anyone who has lived longer than I have in these parts. The Archbishop's father, D. P. MacDonald, died young. He was a great businessman, building Long John into the biggest whisky company in Scotland. Then Colonel Willie and his brother Jack, still only in their twenties, were landed with running a major company without the knowledge or any real interest in doing so. And now, finally, the Archbishop's nephew, Major Andrew, had passed over control of the company. It has been difficult for the family. Too many distilleries, Prohibition in America after the last war and hefty taxes had taken their toll, and now it's forbidden to sell whisky in Great Britain as the grain is needed for food.

I shiver. I'm feeling the cold.

The Archbishop rises. He stretches, and then clears the plates, pokes the fire and puts on more peat.

'I have to confess now, Father,' I say.

'Then we'll be needing a cup of tea. I fancy, by the look of you, that there's still a twist or two to come,' he says. He smiles at me and walks stiffly across to the sink, not too nimble himself these days.

I close my eyes, gathering what strength I have left, and the Archbishop talks while the kettle boils. 'When I used to come here with my older brother Willie, we were all fit and strong,' he says. 'I remember the big stone, must have weighed about half a hundredweight, sitting below that oak tree at the back of the big field by the track over to Polnish. The challenge was to heft it over a branch about seven feet off the ground. No visiting young man ever passed the spot without giving it a try, did they? Willie and I never managed it, although your lad Angus did it with ease, first with his left and then with his right hand! He was the strongest man in Lochaber in his day. And I remember Mairi once proudly telling me that her Sandy and young Donald Peter heaved it over before they went off to Gallipoli.'

I feel a surge of pride, thinking of those fine young men. But both dead now.

The storm lamp is guttering a bit. The Archbishop puts a cup of tea down on the kist beside my bed. 'Where's the paraffin kept?' he asks. 'I'd better fill the light.'

'It's around the back of the house, by the grist mill,' I reply. 'You'll only find an inch or two in it; Louise just about emptied it yesterday.'

Laboriously he pulls on his boots and heads out, no doubt thankful that this isn't the sort of problem they have in Edinburgh these days.

It's now or never, I tell myself, as I await his return.

He's soon back with the tin. 'You've a few hours of fuel left for the lamp and then you'll be out.'

'I'm sorry that my confession has been such a long time coming,' I say. 'It's an unforgivable sin I've been living with. I need to get it out.'

'Don't you worry, Donald John. My chair is comfortable and the fire is fine. You'll see if I start nodding off.'

How will I be able to tell him the truth? That I loved another woman. That I have lived a lie? What will he think of me?

I take a deep breath and tell him everything. How Linde saved my life, about our blossoming friendship as I walked her and Anja to the camp, my attraction to her which I failed to conceal, my conflicting emotions, knowing that she was my prisoner and yet wanting more from her.

'Archbishop, I wanted Linde and had every intention of being intimate with her.'

I pause, but the Archbishop's expression is inscrutable. 'I've been consumed with guilt ever since. I didn't commit adultery but I told her I loved her. And I did. I truly felt a passion that I had never known. I sought ways for us and the child to escape together. She's the reason I stayed longer out there and didn't return to Morag and the children.'

'Do you know where she is now?'

I close my eyes. My mind and body seem to be shutting down, but I gather my strength and blurt out, 'She's dead. Drowned. My blatant feelings for her, which had been obvious for all to see, and my visits to the camp labelled her a traitor . . . and for that she was murdered . . . by the other women.' My voice drops to a whisper. 'Or perhaps she was murdered by me. I feel a great sense of guilt that I am to blame. Let God decide.'

I have been talking for ages and I am as weak as a child now. But I have, at last, made my confession. 'Forgive me, Father, for I have sinned.'

I wait for the Archbishop's reaction. He does not seem shocked; I expect he has heard much worse in his fifty years of hearing confessions.

He looks me straight in the eye and with great clarity and warmth utters these words: 'I don't judge you, Donald John; that is for God to do. But I am able to forgive your sins in Our Lord's name.'

Immediately, I am filled with a profound sense of relief and peace. We say an Act of Contrition together and he instructs me to say the Rosary tomorrow, when I have a quiet moment. I wonder whether I should tell Morag about Linde after all. But our prayer together is my last recollection as I fall into a deep sleep.

Chapter 33

Donald John, South Africa, 1901

The following days were grim – a whirlwind of emotions. I'd escaped a court-martial, but I blamed myself for Linde's death, and Anja was now an orphan. It was the worst time of my life, compounded by constant skirmishes with the enemy, mammoth back-breaking rides and endless rain.

We'd been on patrol for several days and were camped up at Quaagafontein, about eight miles from Zastron. Everyone was exhausted and ready to head back to Aliwal. I remember the date as the nineteenth of September, because it was Sheena's birthday. (Morag never let the occasion pass without a cake and a candle and a toast to our daughter in Canada. I wondered if she'd been able to buy some flour and sugar.) It had been pouring constantly, but that night the skies had cleared a little, and it was bitterly cold.

The solitary sentry post was up on a bushy knoll some two hundred yards from our camp. I was on duty with young Christie from nine until eleven. It was almost ghostly as we stared at the pale moon in the ink-black sky.

Just before change-over I was sure I heard the snap of a stick being broken. 'Did you hear that, Christie?' I whispered.

Christie had heard nothing. I listened carefully for a few more seconds, but there was only silence. Shortly afterwards we were relieved by our replacements and turned in.

I woke with a start to the sound of gunfire and chaos. Groggy from deep sleep, I stumbled from my tent with my rifle. I saw with horror that the tents pitched closer to the hill were having volley after volley poured into them. I caught glimpses of the Boer as they reloaded and fired again and again. The noise and sensation were overwhelming. I shouted for the others to hurry, trying to be heard over the tremendous quantities of rifle shot, bullets passing amongst us, flashes in the darkness, the yells of the Dutch, the workers crying out, and Captain Semphill and the colonel barking orders. Panic-stricken horses and mules were now galloping wildly amongst us, having broken free from their halters. It was a truly hellish din, a combination of sounds that would haunt those of us who survived for years.

There were three of us in a row, bootless, blinking in the dark as rifle flares blinded us and shadows seemed to emerge and then disappear on all sides. We didn't know where the enemy was; every time I fired, I dreaded hitting one of our own. I recklessly risked a couple of shots but the Boer were right amongst us. McLennan was thrown back, his arm flung against mine as he went down; he'd been shot in the face from only yards away. Christie staggered past, clutching his chest, and collapsed, crying out for his mother. Semphill was shouting, 'Regroup! Regroup!' from my left, trying to organise a counter-attack. Then, briefly, came the chatter of our Maxim as it got going, but it was immediately silenced.

Munro and I decided to bolt towards Semphill, but as I went forward I heard a gasp. I turned around and he, too, was down. Then, stumbling over the rocks in my bare feet, I saw the flare from a gun and, somehow, just knew it was for me. There was a massive thump as the bullet hit my thigh, twisted me sideways and threw me on my side. The shot must have been fired from no more than ten yards away. I put my hand down and felt a gaping hole and the horrible, sticky sensation of blood pumping out. I jammed my hat over the gash and lay still.

For a few minutes more, the battle raged all about me. Then the gunfire petered out and only the groans from the injured and excited chatter amongst our assailants could be heard. I tried to call out, but my mouth was as dry as sand; only a croak came. Paraffin lamps were being lit and the Boer were prowling around, checking who was injured. They scoured the camp, gathering everything they could lay their hands on: food, even our boots and watches.

A light was shone in my face and I could just make out a perspiring lad, young enough to be my son, calling out to the others that this one was alive. He gave me some water.

'Where are you from?' he asked in perfect English.

'Scotland ... from the mountains in the north,' I mumbled.

He said he was Scottish, too, a MacDonald. He helped me into a comfortable position with my leg supported up on a rock and ripped up a shirt which he tied around my thigh to staunch the blood flow. He gave me a strip of biltong to grit my teeth into as he pulled bits of cloth out of my wound and bathed it.

'Thank you, thank you,' I murmured. I knew he was

saving my life, that I would have bled to death. Did he really say he was Scottish? A MacDonald? Was I delirious? I asked him to repeat his name.

'MacDonald,' he said, 'Dennis MacDonald.'

I was astonished. I gripped his arm, and he moved his head close to mine to hear me. 'I'm a MacDonald. We're the same clan, probably from the same area of Scotland.' I paused. 'What the hell are you doing fighting for the Boer?'

He started talking now. I had touched a sore point. He had been farming peacefully, keeping out of the war, but then the British arrived at his house and took his horses. A week later, more soldiers arrived and drove off his sheep and cattle. He immediately joined the Boer Commando to fight to get his property back.

I repeated, 'Dennis, Dennis MacDonald.' I wouldn't forget this man's name.

He shook me by the hand and patted me on the shoulder. 'Good luck,' he said. 'I hope you make it.'

The Boer finally headed off with as many of the horses as they could round up, our Armstrong gun and large quantities of ammunition. I remember the sound of wild dogs howling in the distance and wondered if they would be brave enough to come into the camp. There were groans and occasional words from others. I doubted they'd found a saviour as attentive as Dennis MacDonald to patch them up. My wound throbbed terribly; in the dark I couldn't see if it was still bleeding but I could feel that it was an awful, sticky mess down there.

The night dragged on. I kept thinking I was having a nightmare and would wake up with a feeling of relief, but it was not to be. How could things have gone so badly? Had the sentries fallen asleep? Why, in God's name, was there only one sentry post instead of the normal three?

So many in my regiment were dead: it had been a blood-bath. Thirteen Lovat Scouts and seven members of the Artillery had been killed in the attack; their bodies were left at Quaagafontein to be buried there.

Some of our men must have sped off to find Lord Lovat. He and his squadron had been camped several miles away, and they arrived at dawn, followed by the Connaught Rangers and the medical team. Unfortunately, the medics had no morphine with them; it was in short supply here and was only available in hospitals. There followed a pain-ful journey for the survivors to Aliwal North although I remembered little of it as I was, mercifully, unconscious for most of it.

The Indian medics were skilled and caring. They insisted I drink water and sup bowls of liquidised mealies, and watched intently to make sure I did so. There were four of us in the wagon when we set off, but two died on the way to Aliwal and were buried out in the veld. I overheard an Irish soldier calling the convoy 'the train of death'.

My mind was on my family all the time. I was deter-mined to live, to get home, although I realised with a crush-ing sadness what a burden I would be, a cripple for the rest of my days. I had wondered if my wife would stay with me more than a few times recently, and now I would be completely useless. If word got back to her about Linde from Scouts who had returned with the First Contingent then she'd be off to Arisaig before I got home. And who would blame her? But Morag was resilient. She was strong, kind, capable. I prayed that she would do everything she could to hold things together. I thought of Linde, too, but tried to blank that out and think instead of the young girl and her future. Surely Mrs Fawcett would fulfil her promise?

It was the evening before we were due to reach the camp. The mules had been taken out of their traces, and I could hear the canteen workers preparing dinner. An Indian medic was bathing my wound with an iodine and alcohol mixture, which stung like hell. He was gentle and apologetic throughout the procedure. 'Sorry, sahib, sorry, sahib,' he said over and over.

It must have been his tenderness and kindness that set me off because I began to cry like a baby. My body, curled up on its side, shook with convulsions and tears streamed down my face, soaking the rolled-up jacket that had been placed under my head. The trauma of the last few weeks had made me vulnerable. The hideous images in my head of Linde drowning, Anja, alone, fighting for her life, Morag shouting at me, rejecting me, my leg rotting – everything was whirling around my mind.

It was all over in ten minutes. The medic fussed over me, hugely concerned that he was the cause of my grief. I wiped my eyes and reassured him. 'I'm sorry,' I said. 'I'm just overcome with . . . everything.'

We arrived at the army hospital at dawn. The artery wasn't bleeding, the doctors decided, but they were worried about releasing the tourniquet. The Boer MacDonald had done a good job. It was clear to them that my leg had been completely destroyed and they would have to amputate. They gave me a massive dose of morphine before the surgery, but I remained conscious. I fought wildly with the medics holding me down as I heard the rasp of the saw cutting through my thighbone.

The operation to remove my leg didn't go well and infection quickly set in. The stump was festering and the doctor was worried I'd get gangrene. My temperature rocketed, and I was delirious, constantly bathed in sweat, as weak as a kitten. Random images flitted across my mind: Morag cradling a lamb, the old Boer farmer's contorted face as he squeezed the trigger, Linde's pale blue eyes, dead children, row upon row of bell tents and burning farms.

Lieutenant Kenny Macdonald was in and out of the medical station constantly, having promised the captain he'd look after me, and, seeing my rapidly worsening state, took it upon himself to get me on a hospital train to Cape Town. The Connaught Rangers priest was summoned and I was given the last rites before I went. I was barely aware of the Holy Water being sprinkled on my face. I was oddly amused by this, feeling as though my mind was completely detached from my body. I pictured myself being lowered into a grave and stones being piled up as the priest led prayers. Lieutenant Macdonald said he would write to the captain right away, telling him what had happened. He departed with some comforting words about meeting me at the Highland Games in Portree to keep my spirits up.

I was stretchered onto the train and we set off for Cape Town. The young officer accompanying me seemed convinced I would die on the journey and jotted down Morag's details in his notebook. I pictured a War Office clerk at his desk in London typing his tenth standard two-line telegram of the day, informing yet another widow that her husband had fallen bravely in action and offering her condolences.

But I survived, and two days later, with the benefit of a telegram in advance and an introductory letter from Lieutenant Macdonald, I found myself aboard Bullough's *Rhouma* and receiving the best of care in comfortable surroundings. There was a doctor on board, who had access to plenty of medicine that was not available to the rest of the Army, and after a rough week, I realised I was beginning to make a strong recovery. I thought of the poor blighters in their understaffed and poorly equipped hospital tents as I sat in a deckchair overlooking Table Mountain, liveried crew members bringing me lemonade. Two lovely nurses helped me to get used to my crutches, and after a further two weeks I was growing pretty nimble and could hobble around the deck unaided. But it was another two months before I was declared strong enough to travel home. I secured a berth on the HMS *St Andrew*, was taken back to Glasgow, and then put on the train home to Lochailort.

Morag and the children met me in Fort William. I was nervous about seeing her, but her unhappiness about my staying out seemed to have been swept aside as she took control of the situation, in her inimitable way. She was onto the train and into my sleeper cabin in seconds, sitting on the bunk and taking me in her arms.

'I'm so glad to see you, my dear,' she whispered, 'to be taking you home. I've been counting the moments.' She stroked my hair. It was she who was crying now.

On hearing these words my spirits soared. I began to believe that everything was going to be all right.

Captain MacDonald was there, too, with my friends from the First Contingent. He'd organised a welcoming party and we processed to the Station Hotel for lunch. The captain and I had a quiet moment together. He took me aside and told me, with that wry smile of his, to put my best foot forward. Then he leant forward and whispered, 'And never a word about the girl, not a word. Leave all that in South Africa.'

Later, Morag and I sat together, holding hands and talking of many things, trivial and otherwise, on the train to Lochailort. She admitted she had been nervous, even frightened of having me back, and of what our life ahead had in store. 'Reading your letters,' she admitted, 'I could tell you weren't the man I'd said goodbye to.'

Squeezing her hand, I looked her in the eye and said, 'I'm back with you now, darling. For good.'

Chapter 34

Donald John, Ardnish, 1944

I awake, last of the household, to hear Morag quizzing the Archbishop. *Is he all right? Did you finish your conversation?*

The Archbishop is evading the stream of questions and trying to catch my eye. 'Morning, Donald John. Rested, are we?'

I nod, relieved with the unburdening of the night before. 'Feeling quite strong, actually,' I reply. It's true; I feel a strange calm now, and the pain in my chest has abated.

Angus comes in and announces, 'Your cow's gone, Mother. I can see her hoof prints in the snow. Heading over to Laggan, I reckon. Shall I go and find her after breakfast?'

There is a lengthy, convoluted conversation among them all. The Archbishop needs to catch the train at eleven thirty, so Louise and Angus will go with him and then get some provisions from 'Angie the shop' at Polnish, and Morag will retrieve the wayward cow. Mairi will be weaving next door but promises to drop in from time to time. Broch will keep me company.

Morag is wrestling with leaving me, but I know she wants to get outside, and of course she needs to get the cow. I reassure them I'll be fine on my own, that they should all take the chance of some fresh air.

Morag looks relieved. 'Angus, will you get the pony saddled up? The Archbishop can ride him as far as the landslide and we can load him up on the return.'

There's a bustle in the house as tea is brought over to me and the others dig out boots and hats and scarves and gloves. They talk about the change in the weather and how they hope it will hold for the day.

The Archbishop and I shake hands and, a bit gushingly, I thank him for coming. Both of us have tears in our eyes; we know it's the last time we will meet.

Finally, they are all gone. Peace, perfect peace.

I lie back and doze, reflecting on my confession and savouring the sense of contentment it has given me, but suddenly Broch stands, her ears pricked. Someone is out there. I strain to hear.

'Hello?' I call out, my voice sounding hoarse. 'Is that you, Mairi?'

There is a faint tap on the door.

'Come in,' I say.

The door opens, and there, framed in the doorway, is a woman. Tall, slim, with long, braided fair hair.

'Linde? Is that you, Linde?' I whisper, feeling my eyes well up with tears.

'No, Donald John. It's me, Anja.' She approaches the bed. I lift my hands to hers as she bends to kiss my forehead. Then she embraces me.

We look carefully at each other for a few moments. She is smiling. I am searching for similarities to the child I knew a lifetime ago.

'My God, I thought it was your mother coming to take me to the next world,' I whisper.

She sits by my bed and takes my hand. She reaches into her rucksack and pulls out a crumpled slouch hat. 'Look, it's yours. See the tartan patch?' She puts it on. 'Do you remember me wearing this as we walked across the veld? Because I do, vividly, even though I was so young. I've worn it from time to time over the years, too, especially when I'm on a horse. When I was at the camp at Aliwal, a gravedigger brought it to me. He told me you'd left it on my mother's grave. He said it would be stolen.'

'How kind of him,' I manage to say.

'I can only stay a little while,' she says. 'The men say the tide is turning and the boat will get stranded on the sand.'

Anja seems comfortable being with me and my heart swells with happiness. Once again I picture her as a young girl, holding her mother's and my hands as we walk along. Even as a ten-year-old she had her mother's athletic stride, easy laugh and delight in the simplest things. I squeeze her hand tightly.

'I have your letter,' she says, rummaging in her bag again. She pulls out a creased piece of paper, torn from my army notebook. 'Look, I've read it so often that it's become almost impossible to make out the words. It comes with me everywhere. Do you remember writing it?'

'Of course I do,' I reply.

'It's lovely. I'll read it to you.'

To my darling Anja,
I now need to leave you. Soldiers have come to take me back to the camp. It breaks my heart to go. Over the last

month you and your mother have become very precious to me. I pray that your fever has passed and you recover fully. I am leaving you to live with a lovely woman who will bring you up as her daughter.

There will not be a week, a day, an hour that I will not think of you and wish to be with you. Your mother's death will be mourned by us both, and I will love her until my last breath.

I was very touched and proud to get to know you and your mother in difficult times. I will remain forever like a father to you in my heart.

Your loving Donald John Gillies, Ardnish.

Having Anja read my own words from all those years ago moves me to tears. I need time to compose myself, and she seems to understand when I ask her to make us some tea.

I've always been emotional and prone to shedding tears. I remember composing every sentence of that letter, writing 'Ardnish' after my name and wondering why I was doing that. But, deep down, I had always known. It was in the unlikely case Anja might one day come to find me.

'What on earth are you doing here?' I finally remember to ask.

'I'm a senior radio operator for the Dutch SOE, here on a course at Roshven House. The Resistance in Holland is weak now, but there is a new drive to build it up. There are forty Dutch men up here, training to be parachuted back into the country. I am the only woman. I was talking to Peter Blackburn in his garden. He was digging out the last of his turnips for his cattle and he mentioned Ardnish as we were talking. I couldn't believe it. I asked him if he'd just said "Ardnish", and he said yes and pointed over here.

'So I asked if the name Donald John Gillies meant anything to him and he replied it certainly did. He told me you were an old family friend and had helped to build Roshven House. I had your hat in my Nissen hut, so I showed it to him. He said, "That will be his. Look – the Fraser tartan. Donald John was a Lovat Scout." Then he pointed over the water to here, Peanmeanach. We could see smoke coming out of a chimney. I was so excited, I could hardly believe it.'

'Did he not wonder why you had the hat?' I ask.

'Oh, I just brushed it off, told him our family knew you in South Africa. But ... he told me you weren't very well. So I asked one of the army boys for a lift across the loch and here I am!'

I am so relieved that Morag and the others aren't here. Anja and I wouldn't have been able to talk like this.

'Tell me about your life,' I say. 'I've prayed for years that you were all right.'

Anja begins her tale. She is very open and frank. 'I've been lucky. After the Treaty of Vereeniging in 1902, the woman who took me in, Roos, took me to her farm just as her husband, Dolf – he was a gentle giant of a Boer – was released from the internment camp in Ceylon. They got money to rebuild the farm buildings and to buy cattle. They'd had only the one child, a girl who died in the camp, and so they adopted me. I was so lucky. But my new parents were quite old and both died before I was twenty-five. I inherited the farm, but then decided to go to university in Amsterdam so I sold the place. I now have a lovely Dutch husband and two teenage girls in London. We all moved to Britain in 1939, just before the war broke out.'

'Thank God,' I murmur. 'When I left I feared the worst for you. I hated not knowing what might happen to you. After I left you, I lost my leg in battle a few days later. That was a period in my life that changed everything for me.'

'Oh, my goodness,' she gasps.

I gesture across to the corner where my wooden limb is propped against the wall, leather straps trailing down. I don't want to recount the whole story to her and am rescued by the sound of the door opening. There, in the light reflecting off the snow, stands Morag, with the others behind her. Her mouth is wide open in astonishment as she looks from the visitor to me.

There is a moment's silence until Anja approaches my wife with a beaming smile. 'You must be Morag. I've heard all about you from Donald John.'

My wife is lost for words and my family are on their most polite behaviour as this striking woman talks nine-teen to the dozen about how we'd met in South Africa, how I'd saved her and her mother's lives, and thank God, now we have met again thanks to Peter Blackburn.

It is only a minute or two, however, before a couple of soldiers appear in the doorway and tell Anja that she must leave now. The tide is going out and they don't want to be stranded here.

Anja takes my hand, kisses me on the forehead, and quietly says farewell. As she leaves she turns to give me one last lingering look before she strides off through the door-way. My eyes are welling, but a coughing fit saves me from blubbing like a baby.

Everyone is talking at once. *Who was she? How did she know we lived here?* All eyes are on me.

'Morag, can I have a quiet word?' I whisper.

Louise, Angus and Mairi instinctively know to retreat next door to Mairi's, and they leave us alone.

I open my mouth to tell my wife all, but no words come. My head falls forward and my body collapses, as if all my energy has been sucked out. I suddenly feel more tired than I have ever felt before.

Chapter 35

Morag, Ardnish, 1944

A few moments ago, my husband looked so content. It was as if he had found peace. But now he is coughing hard. His chest is full of phlegm which is drowning him. I can see that he is struggling to breathe. I jump to my feet and rush next door to get the others.

We all return, and I sit on the bed, holding his hand. Mairi kneels on the stone floor beside us, hands pressed together as she prays. Louise stands close by, tears pouring down her face.

Then our son says the last rites, '*O Dhia an Tiarna*', as Donald John passes.

I kiss him and gently pull the blanket over his head, whispering, 'He was a good man.'